My Perfect Enemy

WHITECAP

A SINGLE FATHER SMALL-TOWN ROMANCE

JESSICA PRINCE

Tempting Sophia
Enticing Daphne
Charming Fiona

<u>STANDALONE TITLES:</u>
One Knight Stand
Chance Encounters
Nightmares from Within

<u>DEADLY LOVE SERIES:</u>
Destructive
Addictive

<u>**THE COLORS NOVELS:**</u>
Scattered Colors
Shrinking Violet
Love Hate Relationship
Wildflower

<u>**THE LOCKLAINE BOYS (a LOVE HATE RELATIONSHIP spinoff):**</u>
Fire & Ice
Opposites Attract
Almost Perfect

<u>**THE PEMBROOKE SERIES (a WILDFLOWER spinoff):**</u>
Sweet Sunshine
Coming Full Circle
A Broken Soul

<u>**CIVIL CORRUPTION SERIES**</u>
Corrupt
Defile
Consume
Ravage

<u>**GIRL TALK SERIES:**</u>
Seducing Lola

Wrong Side of the Tracks
Stay With Me
Out of the Darkness
The Second Time Around
Waiting for Forever
Love to Hate You
Playing for Keeps
When You Least Expect It
Never for Him

REDEMPTION SERIES

Bad Alibi

Crazy Beautiful

Bittersweet

Guilty Pleasure

Wallflower

Blurred Line

Slow Burn

Favorite Mistake

THE PICKING UP THE PIECES SERIES:

Picking up the Pieces

Rising from the Ashes

Pushing the Boundaries

Worth the Wait

Discover Other Books by Jessica

WHITECAP SERIES
Crossing the Line
My Perfect Enemy

WHISKEY DOLLS SERIES
Bombshell

Knockout

Stunner

Seductress

Temptress

HOPE VALLEY SERIES:
Out of My League
Come Back Home Again
The Best of Me

Whitecap Playlist

"Carry on Wayward Son" by Kansas

"Simple Man" by Lynyrd Skynyrd

"Bad Moon Rising" Creedence Clearwater Revival

"Can't You See" by The Marshall Tucker Band

"Free Bird" by Lynyrd Skynyrd

"House of the Rising Sun" by The Animals

"Burnin' for You" by Blue Öyster Cult

"Paint It, Black" by The Rolling Stones

"All Along the Watchtower" by Jimi Hendrix

"Gimme Shelter" by The Rolling Stones

"Slow Ride" by Foghat

"(Don't Fear) The Reaper" by Blue Öyster Cult

"In-A-Gadda-Da-Vida" by Iron Butterfly

"Whole Lotta Love" by Led Zeppelin

“Black Dog” by Led Zeppelin
“One Thing Right” by Marshmello and Kane Brown

One

LUNA

THE BAR SMELLED like stale beer and cheap whiskey that would rot your gut if you drank more than a few sips. Half the floor was covered in crushed peanut shells while the other half was sticky with spilled drinks that hadn't been mopped up properly. The stools were wobbly, the vinyl seat cushions cracked or torn, the stuffing popping out like a busted tin of biscuits, and every drink was served in a thin, cheap, clear plastic cup, not a literal glass in sight.

It was a dive, barely half a step up from a pit, but it was absolutely perfect for me, given my mood the past couple months. Truth was, I wasn't feeling much better than the shit making my shoes stick to the grimy floor.

This wasn't where I was supposed to be, especially at eleven o'clock on a Wednesday night. And I *absolutely* wasn't supposed to be slinging drinks behind the bar, and not only because I didn't have the first clue what the hell I was doing.

I'd been my own boss up until a few months ago, living the dream most people had of running their own company. I worked as a freelance graphic and web designer, and I'd been damn good at it.

I'd had nothing to complain about. I was riding high and living my best life. Then everything started going downhill. Business had started to slow down once I'd tapped the local market. The change had been gradual at first, but then the pace picked up, going from a deluge to a steady stream to barely more than a trickle.

That was the thing about small towns, the client base wasn't very big. Everyone in town did their best to support me, but there was only so much need for a graphic designer. I'd attempted to expand my client base, putting my name out in the bigger cities nearby, but people in those cities tended to go with larger firms. No one wanted to take a shot on a self-taught designer when they could have someone with that coveted degree.

I ran through my nest egg faster than expected, trying to keep my business afloat, holding out hope that things would start looking up. Of course, hindsight being the bitch it was, I was able to look back and see all the things I'd done wrong—like bail my mom out every damn time she needed money instead of putting my foot down, or buying a house I couldn't really afford just because it was my dream home. But focusing on that wouldn't do anything but make me feel even worse than I already did.

Determined to climb out of the quicksand that threatened to suck me under, I'd pulled myself up by the bootstraps and found work wherever I could. Well, *almost* wherever I could. There were bars and restaurants in my hometown of Whitecap where I could have gotten a job, but I was still struggling with the embarrassment of my business going under and wasn't quite ready for the people in my life to know just yet. That meant I'd gone one town over to this shithole, all because none of my friends would set foot in this place, and applied for the bartending gig.

I could have gone to my best friend, Cheyanne, who still worked part-time at Warren's General Store despite having her own growing pottery business. She'd mentioned more than once that orders were coming in faster than she could handle and how she was considering bringing on help, but my pride had prevented me from telling her the truth.

Or I could have gone to her fiancé, Trent, who was opening a branch of the security firm he'd worked at back in Hope Valley, Virginia before making the move to the opposite coast to be with his woman. Even my friend Monica, who owned Drip, the local coffee shop, would have happily taken me on. But going to any of them would have meant admitting that, while they were thriving, I'd failed colossally. I just couldn't do it.

Even though I *hated* this job. Even though the only drink I had any clue how to mix was a margarita . . . something the drunks, criminals, and outlaws who made up this place's clientele weren't too big on. Even though my boss was a lecherous, sleazy pig, I couldn't bring myself to tell my loved ones the truth. Not while the shame still festered.

It was on that thought, while I was in the process of scooping up the empty plastic cups on the bar top and throwing them in the trashcan beside me, that the door swung open with the arrival of another customer, bringing the grand total for the night so far to a whopping ten.

Thank the good Lord I was the only one on the schedule for tonight because the tips so far were laughable, and if I'd had to split them with someone else, that laughter might have turned into tears. Not that these drunk wastes-of-space were likely to tip well in the first damn place.

The guy who just walked into the bar looked like he belonged in this place just as much as I did, maybe even less so. He wore pressed slacks and a crisp white button-down. The shirt was open at his throat and the cuffs of his sleeves were folded to his elbows, revealing thick, veined forearms, the skin tanned a lovely golden caramel from the sun.

His gaze remained downcast as he moved through the bar. He didn't seem to notice the stares he was getting from the regulars or the fact that his expensive dress shoes were making a horrifying slurping sound with each step he took on the disgusting floor as he made his way toward the bar.

It didn't take insightful bartender juju to realize this dude wasn't in a good way as he closed in on the bar and hefted himself onto an empty stool. It was obvious by the slump in his shoulders, the slight bow in his back, and the simple fact that he was *here* that screamed the guy was having a pretty rough day.

I started in his direction, ready to save him from making his evening even worse by sticking around a place like this. This crowd wasn't really hip on the clean-cut suit and tie types. Hell, I wasn't sure they were hip on just plain *clean*, so this man stuck out like a sore thumb. "Hey there, listen—"

He cut me off midsentence. "Scotch, neat," he said on a grunt. "Macallan if you've got it."

The bark of laughter that erupted from my chest jolted the man into finally looking at me for the first time since he entered the bar. "Sorry, but have you bothered to look around at where you are?" I asked once I'd gained control of my hilarity. "This look like the kind of place that carries Macallan to you?"

His head swiveled on his neck, taking in the rundown bar—for the first time if the shock in his gaze was anything to go by. Instead of shooting up and hightailing it out like I'd expected, he finally looked back at me and asked, "Then what do you have?"

"Stuff not even suitable for the bottom shelf," I informed him honestly. "That is, unless you're looking to burn a hole in the lining of your stomach."

He let out a sigh that sounded like it held the weight of the world. "Fine. I'll just take a beer then. Whatever you have on tap."

The beer wasn't much better than the liquor, but I figured I'd done my part in trying to run this guy off. Wasn't my fault it didn't take. Hopefully the designer shoes and expensive watch meant he'd be a better tipper than the snaggle-toothed patron farther down the bar. Last night, that guy had tipped me with an expired coupon to a sandwich shop that had gone out of business back in the 90's.

Moving to the tap, I flipped over one of the slightly larger plastic cups we kept for beer, and pulled the brew that tasted the least like piss. "Here you go," I said as I set the cup down in front of him. I shrugged my shoulders when he looked from the cup to me in dismay, then pointed at the beer. "Hey, man, what did you expect? This is a dive. We serve rot gut and cheap beer in plastic cups.

But my guess is you didn't walk in here for the ambience, so cheap or not, that'll do the job you need it to do."

With another sigh, this one more weary than heavy, he lifted the cup and took a huge gulp, only wincing slightly at the aftertaste. "It'll do," he said before taking another pull. "And I'll open a tab."

My gaze darted around the bar one more time. Most everyone had gone back to minding their own business, drowning their sorrows in cheap booze, but there were two or three guys who looked like they were in the mood to start some shit. "You sure you want to do that?"

His brow furrowed and I noticed this man wasn't just attractive like I'd initially expected, but downright *hot*. Expressive, arched brows rested over the most distinctive blue-gray eyes I'd ever seen. As he looked at me, I was reminded of the morning fog rolling over the choppy sea outside my bedroom window, or the angry crash and slam of the waves on an overcast day.

A fringe of thick, dark lashes encircled those beautiful eyes, leading down to cheekbones sharp enough to slice through a wedge of Manchego cheese. His Grecian nose was perfectly straight, and his powerful square jaw was coated with a five o'clock shadow that only accentuated his classic good looks. In fact, he was so damn attractive, I wanted to lean across the bar so I could drag my tongue up the column of his thick throat.

His Adam's apple bobbed, pulling me from my ogling, as he asked, "Why wouldn't I?" Yeah, this guy *definitely* didn't belong in this bar, but I couldn't say I was bummed he'd come waltzing in. Out of all the shitholes in all the towns, that man came walking into mine.

"Oh, I don't know. Maybe because a couple of our regulars look like they want to see how well their fists will fit in your face." And it really would have been a shame to ruin such a perfect face.

He didn't bother to look around that time, he simply picked up the plastic cup and drank most of the beer in it in two big gulps. "They can try if they want. They won't have much luck, though."

There was something in the way he said it, in the blitheness of his tone, that made me think he wasn't just blowing smoke or trying to make himself seem like more of a badass than he was. Something told me this man could hold his own in a fight, and, given his dark mood, might actually welcome one. I let my gaze linger over his broad, rounded shoulders and the thickness of his biceps beneath his expensive shirt. From what I could tell, his chest was defined and wide, his whole physique giving the impression of strength and making me think he was more than capable of holding his own in a fight, even with these wastes of humanity.

"Well, all right then. It's your funeral," I said, biting

back a smile as I pointed at the now empty cup. "Another?"

"Please."

I moved back to the tap and pulled another, depositing it in front of the sexy stranger. "If you don't mind me asking, what brings a guy like you to a place you absolutely don't belong, drinking beer only a step or two up from piss water?"

He'd been in the process of taking another drink during my question and proceeded to choke on said piss water. Once he was able to breathe again, he took the time to look me over the same way I'd done to him just seconds ago, only he was blatantly unrepentant in his obviousness. For some reason that made my skin heat pleasantly. This man knew who he was, what he liked, and didn't seem to care about showing that. I had to admit, I'd never met a man so sure of himself before, and I was drawn to him, almost intoxicatingly so.

His lips hooked up into a smirk. "You sure do hold your place of employment in high regard."

I gave my shoulders a small shrug, pulling the white hand towel from where I'd tucked it into the string of the apron tied around my waist and began giving the bar top a scrub, not that it would do much good. I was starting to think the whole building was made entirely of grime and bodily fluids I didn't want to think about. "It is what it is.

I mean, you can look around and see for yourself this place isn't exactly boasting five stars on *Yelp*, so what's the point in lying, right?"

"Can't polish a turd and call it a diamond."

I let out a surprised laugh at the guy's unexpected statement. "Exactly." Resting my forearms onto the part of the bar I'd just cleaned, I leaned in close to the stranger who had me all kinds of enthralled. "You haven't answered my question," I said in a teasing, somewhat flirty tone.

He arched a single brow as he brought the cheap beer to his lips and drank, his throat working on a deep swallow. *Damn*, who knew a throat could be sexy? "Remind me what that question was."

"Why'd you pick this hell mouth, of all places, to grab a drink?"

He blew out a breath before reaching up and rubbing at the tension in the back of his neck. "Seemed as good a place as any to get shitfaced." At my arched look, he let out a chuckle that sounded like velvet over jagged rocks and amended. "Okay, I needed a drink, and this was the first place I passed."

"Bad day?"

He sucked back more beer. "You could say that."

Having been there myself—more than a few times recently—I felt for the man. Heading back over to the tap,

I poured him another drink. "Then this one's on me," I said as I sat it in front of him.

Having finished off beer number two, he lifted the third and shot me a wink that made my insides flutter. "Thanks for this. Fuck bad days, right?"

Truer words had never been spoken.

Two

LUNA

THE STRANGER HAD HUNG around the bar for a few more hours, but had switched to water after that third beer. I was sure he was going to leave at any time, but he didn't. Instead, we'd engaged in conversation whenever I wasn't checking on the other customers or pouring drinks.

Aside from learning he'd had a bad day—without him going into much detail—I'd also learned that he was funny as hell and pretty damn clever. I'd laughed more in the past three hours than I had in months, and it was *really* nice to have my mind taken off all the unhappiness in my life, at least for a little while.

Another thing I'd learned was the man smelled absolutely *incredible*. I'd had trouble placing the familiar smell at first, at least until he'd stepped out of the bar for a few minutes to have a cigar, then it hit me. The leather and cloves scent, the faintest hint of fresh tobacco. I'd spent a small fortune—back when I actually had money—on a candle that smelled like a humidor, and it smelled *exactly* like him. As the night wore on, the desire to lean in and press my face into the guy's neck grew stronger and stronger. And I'd learned I was incredibly attracted to him. That could either be good or bad, depending on one very important circumstance.

You see, I was what all my friends liked to call a seasonal dater. It was a running joke with them that I refused to get involved with any men who lived locally. They thought it was just that I hadn't finished sowing my wild oats yet, and once it was out of my system, I'd join them in settling down and popping out enough babies to form my own family band. But the truth was, that was *never* going to happen.

I'd seen firsthand the devastation heartbreak could wreak on a person, and I had no desire to travel down that road. I'd learned at a young age that Copeland women were cursed when it came to love, and the only way to keep my heart safe was to keep it locked away where no man could get to it.

My grandmother had barely turned nineteen when she met the love of her life, giving her heart to him fully, and when she'd lost him about a decade later, she'd been destroyed. I'd always known my grandmother was a bitter, cynical woman, but it wasn't until I was much older that my mother explained why that was. When my grandfather died, all the best parts of my grandmother had died with him. She'd gone from a woman full of spirit to a cold shell of a person.

"Her heart callused over," Mom used to explain whenever I asked why grandma was so mean. "That's what happens when you never use it."

My mom, on the other hand, was the polar opposite. As if she had worried her own heart would callus, she'd handed it off to any man who gave her a smile and a kind word. She was the kind of woman who didn't know how to function without a man. Her entire existence revolved around whoever she was dating at that time. She poured so much of herself into her relationships there was never enough love left for me. At least until the latest scumbag she'd tied herself to left her heartbroken.

It was during those in-between times she'd remember I existed, but that was only because she needed me to take care of her until she could "get on her feet again." Getting on her feet *always* consisted of finding another man to hook her star to and devoting herself to him completely, to the point she changed everything from her hair to her personality to make him happy.

It never failed that the bloom would eventually fall off the rose, and the cycle would start all over. She'd be dumped, left with nothing because she didn't have a life of her own, and I'd pick up the pieces until she threw me over for a new man. Wash, rinse, repeat.

To make matters worse, the men she went after were no better than the losers I served in this shithole bar night after night. Hell, if this place had been picked up and transported to where I'd grown up, I wouldn't have been surprised to see more than a few "uncles" come wandering in. This place was totally my mom's crowd, a contributing factor to why I hated it so damn much . . . aside from the obvious.

After years and years spent with a mother so consumed by her relationships she forgot her own kid existed, I'd made a promise to myself that I was never *ever* going to fall in love. Which meant hooking up with locals was totally out of the question.

"So, I have to ask," the stranger started as I worked to clear the bar a couple feet away of empty cups and smashed peanut shells, "what the hell are you doing working in a place like this?"

I dusted my hands off on the towel before hooking it back into my apron strings. Grinning slyly, I stretched my arms wide and rested my palms on the counter, leaning in closer to him. "For all you know, these could be my people. Are you saying I don't belong?"

He shook his head and smirked knowingly. "You

belong here just about as much as I do. I know for a fact these aren't your people. Clocked it about a minute after walking in here."

"Oh yeah? Enlighten me." It had been so long since I'd flirted with a man, I'd forgotten how much fun it could be. I would have rather volunteered to have all my teeth ripped out with no anesthesia than flirt with any of the bottom-feeders that frequented this place.

With the stress of everything in my life lately, men hadn't exactly been on my radar. I was too busy panicking that I was dangerously close to losing everything I'd worked my ass off for to even consider a random hookup or casual date. It was nice to be reminded I was still a woman.

He did another one of those up and down perusals. "Well, for starters, you haven't lost any of your teeth to meth just yet."

My head fell back on an uncontrollable belly laugh that lasted long enough to make my ab muscles ache. "Oh man," I wheezed as I wiped tears from my eyes. "Okay, that was a good one."

The stranger was giving me a smile that made my skin tingle with awareness. He had perfectly straight, white teeth. His bottom lip was nice and plump, begging to be bitten. His top lip was just a bit thinner, but had a perfectly shaped cupid's bow I wanted to trace with my tongue. "Then there's the fact your clothes are good quality and don't have any holes in them that weren't put there by design."

So this guy recognized labels as well as I did. Why the hell did I find that so hot? "Another point in your favor. What else?"

"That leaves the most obvious. You're way too damn beautiful for this to be your scene and these your people."

I *tsked* and shook my head as I stood tall and took a couple steps back. "Careful, stranger, or I might start to think you're a judgmental ass who only cares about looks."

It was his turn to laugh as I moved to take care of the other folks in the bar. I looked down at my watch after pouring a shot of whiskey that smelled more like rubbing alcohol for one guy who was, in fact, missing a couple front teeth, noting the hour for the first time since the sexy stranger walked through that door.

"Last call," I shouted from behind the bar to be heard over the crackly music coming out of the jukebox in the corner that was on its last leg. "Finish 'em if you got 'em, then get the hell out."

My command was met with a few unhappy grumbles I ignored as I moved back down the counter to the stranger. He was staring into his water, his expression almost pensive as he slowly turned the plastic cup between his long fingers.

I stopped in front of him, tilting my head to the side. "You good?"

"Hmm?" His head came up at my question. "Oh, yeah. I'm good. Better than I was when I first walked in here, that's for damn sure."

I smiled, feeling that declaration deep in my belly. Working at a place like this, I didn't encounter much nice, especially from someone who looked like he'd just walked off the cover of a magazine. "Well, I'm glad to have been of service." I tipped my chin down to his cup. "Want one more before hitting the road? Maybe something stronger?"

He looked at me for a beat, long enough for my skin to prickle with anticipation, before answering. "That depends."

I lifted my brows, a tiny grin playing on my lips. "On?"

"On what you're doing after this."

Oh damn.

That flutter I'd been feeling in my belly since shortly after he walked in grew in intensity. I'd been getting vibes off the guy all night long, vibes I was feeling myself, but I hadn't been the mood to make the first move. I was totally down for a fun, no-strings night with this guy, however, there was one thing I had to make sure of first.

"You from here?"

I felt a sharp sense of relief when he shook his head. "Not here, but I have a room at a place in the next town."

The next town meant Whitecap, which could potentially spell problems if this guy hadn't clearly been passing through. "You're staying at the Boardwalk Inn?"

Those strange blueish eyes flashed with something that looked like a mixture of excitement and anticipation, and just that brief look had my blood pumping. "Yeah. You know it?"

"I do. I can meet you there once I'm done closing up here. Just give me your room number."

Being friends with the owner of the inn might have posed a problem in regards to privacy if I didn't know her well enough to know she'd already been in bed for the better part of four hours, so I could get in and out without detection.

The guy gave me his room number and rose from his stool, reaching into his back pocket for his wallet. He pulled out a few bills and tossed them onto the bar—far more than what he needed to cover his tab. When I reached for the cash, his hand shot out, his fingers wrapping around my wrist like a cuff. "I didn't get your name."

"You didn't," I confirmed, having no intention of revealing that bit of information. "And I didn't ask for yours." I shot the man a wink. "It's more fun that way."

His chuckle warmed my insides. "All right. I'll play this your way. How long will it take for you to finish up here and get to me?"

Oh *man*, this guy was potent, and I was suddenly eager to throw every single person in here out on their ass so I could lock up and book it back to Whitecap. I gave my head a shake, letting out a long, calming exhale through my nose. "Not long. Less than an hour."

Those incredible lips curved up into another breathtaking smile. "I'll be waiting."

I rolled over, my body feeling sorer than it had in longer than I could remember. My brain felt fuzzy and my eyes felt like sandpaper as I forced them open to take in my surroundings. It took a moment for me to remember what had transpired the night before—or earlier that morning, I guess—but once I did, the soreness suddenly made a whole lot of sense.

The man from the bar, the stranger I refused to trade names with, had rocked my freaking *world*. There had been several instances over the hours he'd worked my body like I was a musical instrument and he was part of the New York Philharmonic where I'd thought I had to have been dreaming. Then he'd nip sharply at my skin with his teeth or give my ass a stinging slap to remind me it was all very, *very* real.

It had been, hands down, the best sexual experience of

my life, and as languid as my body still felt after such an intense workout, it was time to go.

The view from the window told me the sun was just starting to rise. The sky had gone from a deep, dark black to a grayish-purple, announcing the beginning of a new day. In no time, Gloria, my friend who ran the inn, would be awake, and I needed to get out of here before she made her way to the front desk.

If Gloria found out, it would only be a matter of time before that gossip spread like wildfire. As much as I loved her, she didn't know how to keep her mouth shut, and if she caught wind I came back to the inn with a man, I'd be hearing about this particular escapade from pretty much the entire town long after I was ready to put it behind me as a distant memory.

I forced myself from the warm, cozy confines of the bed and padded around the dark room on tiptoes as I searched for the clothes the stranger had ripped off me. I final managed to locate everything and was slipping on my last shoe when the bedside lamp flipped on unexpectedly, startling a yelp out of me as my eyes fought to adjust to the light.

"Sneaking off in the dead of night?"

"More like sneaking off at the crack of dawn," I joked, my lips pulling up into a smirk. "Didn't mean to wake you; sorry about that."

He sat up, the sheets pooling at his waist, revealing a fine-as-hell slab of abs and firm, rounded pecs dusted with just the slightest bit of chest hair. Judging by the faint lines around his eyes when he smiled and the smallest bit of gray at his temples, I would have put the dude was somewhere in his late-thirties or early-forties, but it was obvious by his size and the cut of his muscles that he worked hard to stay in shape, and I couldn't help but ogle. The man really was gorgeous, and the sex-tousled hair only made him that much hotter.

"Nah, it wasn't you. I'm a light sleeper." His lips turned up in a lazy, sleepy grin. "So . . ."

"So . . ." I added on a giggle. "Thanks for, you know."

He arched a single brow. "The orgasms?"

I shook my head on a laugh. "I was going to say thanks for an incredible night, but yours works too."

"Well, you're welcome. And thanks for making a shitty day pretty damn good there at the end."

"It's a gift," I said with a shrug. Reaching down to grab my purse from where I'd dropped it on the antique writer's desk nestled in front of the window, I hooked the strap over my shoulder and moved back to the bed. Leaning down, I brushed my lips gently against his in one last kiss. "Last night was fun. I haven't had a whole lot of that lately, so thank you."

"You sure you have to go?" he asked in a husky voice.

When I pulled back, I noticed his eyes had grown dark and his breathing was heavier; if I didn't leave now, I'd definitely get caught, and that couldn't happen. "Yeah, I do."

"I get it," he said, his voice gentle and quiet. He understood what this was as much as I did: an itch that needed to be scratched, nothing more. "Maybe I'll see you around."

He wouldn't but that was okay. This was the kind of man you couldn't help but want to settle down with, and I was anything but the settling down type. Unable to help myself, I leaned in for one last kiss that he took deeper by grabbing hold of the nape of my neck and sliding his tongue between my lips. By the time we pulled apart, I was out of breath and seriously contemplating saying to hell with the gossip and diving back into bed with him.

But that would only complicate things. And the last thing I needed in my chaotic life was another complication.

"Yeah, maybe," I told him noncommittally. Then I headed for the door, determined to leave the best sex I'd ever had behind me for good.

Three

LUNA

As I sat at my dining room table, my laptop open among the bills and past due notices scattered all around it, panic clutched at my chest, sinking its icy claws deeper and deeper into my heart. The high I'd been riding since that night with my stranger nearly a month ago had just died a tragic and painful death when I tried to be a grown-up and sit down to work on my finances.

Turns out, things were even worse than I'd originally thought. The money I was making at the bar wasn't nearly enough to cover my standard cost of living, even with the few freelance web design jobs I'd been lucky enough to pull in. I'd barely managed to swing my mortgage payment this month, I was a month behind on the electric bill, and the only reason the water was turned back on was because I'd taken every dollar in tips I'd made over the past week and paid down what I owed, putting me only two months behind instead of three.

As stupid as it was—and it had to have been the stupidest thing I'd ever done—I'd been burying my head in the sand for way too long now, choosing to ignore my problems and pretend they didn't exist rather than deal with them. Not my finest choice, I'd admit. Now denial was no longer an option. I was in a hole so deep I could barely see the light above me, illuminating my way out.

I stared at the big, bold, ugly number on the bottom of my computer screen, the one mocking me, revealing my failures, until my vision began to blur. I was quickly running out of options, and the very few I had left held the exact same appeal as making out with a rattlesnake.

But I was a grown-up, damn it, and I had to do what I had to do. This was my dream home, the only place I ever felt I truly belonged, and there was no way in hell I'd lose it.

Pulling in a calming breath, I looked around my own personal piece of heaven, my sanctuary. I'd been in love with the idyllic Cape Cod that sat on a tranquil piece of beach on the edge of town since the very first time I laid eyes on it. With its steep gabled dormers, navy blue shutters, and red front door against wood-shingled siding that had been whitewashed from years and years of sea breeze, it could have been plucked from the pages of one of the countless books I read as a child—the very pages I lost myself in regularly and kept company with, to keep from feeling so damn lonely—and been plopped down right here in my town. As much as I was in love with it from the outside, the inside was even more of a dream with rich, authentic crown molding, wide-plank wood floors, and huge windows overlooking the sea just beyond my backyard.

I knew the moment I saw it that I *had* to live there, I *had* to make it my forever home. It was where I needed to be, so when it came on the market, I knew it was meant to be. I barely gave a second look to the price. Mainly because the number was scary as hell, but also because I wasn't going to let it dissuade me. I made an offer I could *barely* manage and scrawled my name on the paperwork with a flourish on closing day. Now I was at risk of having it taken from me.

I picked up my cellphone from the top of the glaring stack of bills, and scrolled to the very last number I wanted to call.

It took several rings for her to answer, so many I was starting to think I'd end up having to make this request to her voicemail, but at the last possible second, the call connected and my mother's voice carried through the line.

"Luna?"

"Yeah, it's me. Hi, Mom."

She hesitated for a spell before finally saying, "Well this is a surprise," her tone holding no small amount of suspicion. I was deviating from our usual pattern. How things usually worked between us was I didn't bother reaching out because I knew trying to get even the smallest bit of my mother's attention when she had a man in her life was pointless, and she only got in contact with me after she'd been dumped and needed taken care of until her next boyfriend came along.

"Yeah. So, um . . . how are you?" My lips pulled into a thin line at my pathetic attempt at small talk. With how awkward this felt, you'd think I was talking to a complete stranger or an uncomfortable blind date, not the woman who gave birth to me.

"Oh, you know," she hedged. "Same old, same old. How are things with you, dear?"

There wasn't going to be a better opening to say what I needed to say than this, whether I was ready for it or not, so I dove right in. "That's kind of why I'm calling. Things are pretty bad, Mom." It was the first time I'd admitted it out loud to anyone, and a painful lump formed in my throat at the admission. God, I felt like such a failure. That was probably the worst part of this whole mess.

"Oh no." She pulled in a gasp like she was genuinely concerned, in spite of the fact we hadn't spoken in nearly a year. "What's the matter, sweetie? Are you sick?"

"No." I cleared my throat of the knot of shame that had formed, making it difficult to breathe. "It's nothing like that."

"Okay . . . then what's going on? You made it sound so dire."

"Well, it kind of is, Mom. Things with my business . . . they haven't been so great," I confessed, my voice small and broken. "If something doesn't change soon, I'm afraid I might lose my house."

"Oh, honey, you know I'd offer you a place to stay if I could. It's just that Dwight is kind of a private guy, and he's not really big on having a bunch of people in his house."

I bit back the sardonic laughter that wanted to burst forth. Of course, I wasn't surprised in the slightest that the mother of the year on the other end of the call would respond like that. In fact, I'd have been more surprised if dear old Dwight even knew Madeline Copeland had a daughter.

As hard as I tried, I couldn't keep the bitterness and resentment out of my voice as I said, "As much as I appreciate that heartfelt non-offer, that's not what I'm calling to ask." You'd have thought after twenty-nine years of this, it would have stopped hurting so much, but nope. Each interaction left me with a thousand papercuts on my heart that never seemed to heal all the way.

"Then I don't understand—"

I cut her off, spitting the words out at a rapid-fire pace. "It would really help if you could start making payments on the money I've loaned you over the years. I've never pushed you on the matter, and I wouldn't now if I had a choice, but, well, I really need it."

Ten seconds of complete silence followed. I knew because I'd counted. And I also knew in the pit of my stomach that whatever was going to accompany those seconds wasn't going to be good. "Look, Luna, I wish I could help you, honestly, but I can't afford to give you any money. Dwight and I are practically living paycheck to paycheck as it is."

"But I thought you were doing better. Didn't you have a job lined up at that salon once you finished cosmetology school?" *Cosmetology school that* I *paid for*? I thought with a heaping scoop of resentment.

"I've been meaning to talk to you about that." There was no way whatever came after that was going to be good.

"Mom, what did you do?" I asked with exasperation.

"Dwight thought the money would be put to better use if we invested in his friend's business, and I agreed. It was my money, after all. You gave it to me to do with as I wanted, and I wanted to invest it."

"No, I *loaned* it to you so you could enroll in cosmetology school and finally do something with your life," I insisted furiously.

"You never said anything about that money being a loan."

My mouth fell open so fast my jaw popped. "Are you kidding? The agreement was *always* that you would pay the money back I've given you. Not just the loan for school, but for all the times I've bailed you out."

Mom sniffed through the line. "Well I don't remember it that way."

Of course she wouldn't. I squeezed my eyes closed and pulled in a slow, steady inhale, counting to ten before I blew it back out. "You know what, it doesn't matter," I said, trying my best to brush it off. "What happened with the investment? Is there anything from that you could pay me back with?"

More silence. This conversation was swirling around the toilet faster than I could have possibly imagined. "It was a risk, we knew that going in. But if you don't take risks, there's no fun, and what's the point in living if you don't have fun?"

"That's totally fine . . . if you're taking those risks with *your own money*," I shouted, unable to keep my composure. "If I'd known you were going to give it to your waste-of-oxygen boyfriend and his worthless friend, I never would have loaned it to you. I was hoping, for once, you'd use it on something to better yourself so you'd finally stop depending on all those pathetic assholes!"

"You know what?" my mom started on a huff, "I don't have to listen to this. You have no right talking about Dwight like that—"

I cut her off, my voice and fury rising with each word I spoke. "Mom, he's a piece of shit, just like every other man you've ever chosen."

"That's it, I'm done with this conversation. Don't bother calling again until you're ready to apologize."

It would be a cold day in hell before that happened, but she'd already disconnected before I had a chance to tell her that.

My whole body vibrated with rage, my muscles locked so tight I knew my neck and shoulders were going to be killing me tomorrow. I wanted so desperately to wrench my arm back and send my phone crashing into the wall, but I couldn't afford a replacement, so I settled for filling my lungs with air, dropping my head back, and letting it out on a loud, feral yell that grated against my throat like sandpaper and was riddled with every curse word I knew, and some I just came up with on the fly.

"I'd ask if you're okay, but I think the answer to that is pretty obvious."

I let out a startled scream and whipped around in my

seat so fast I fell out of my chair and right onto my ass. "Ow, damn it! Can this night get any worse?"

Cheyanne rushed over to me, extending her hand to help me off the floor. "Shit. Sorry about that. I didn't mean to scare you. I thought you heard me come in, but then you started yelling like something out of a horror movie."

With her help, I climbed off the floor, massaging the ache in my butt cheek with a wince before sitting back down carefully. "Yeah, sorry. I wasn't expecting company." I turned to give her a curious look. "Speaking of, what are you doing here?"

She looked at me like I'd just grown a third eyeball in the middle of my forehead. "Holy shit. You forgot?"

The skin between my brows puckered with an exaggerated frown. "What are you talking about? And where's Renee?" Cheyanne's little girl was probably the closest I'd ever come to being even the slightest bit maternal. She was my little buddy, and I loved seeing her any chance I got, even if I was in the middle of a crisis and I was terrible company.

"She's at home with Trent. It's Margarita Monday, Lu."

I paused, blinking slowly. *Ah, hell.* Margarita Monday had been our tradition for years. One Monday a month we got together, drank margaritas, and laughed, that was it.

One Monday a month everything else was put on the back burner for a few hours, and it was just about two friends spending time together, appreciating the fact we each had someone in our lives who meant something special. It had been my favorite day of the month for years, and the fact it had slipped my mind shocked the hell out of me.

"Shit. I can't believe I forgot."

"You and me both. What the hell is going on, Lu?"

"God, Chey, I don't even know where to start." I buried my face in my hands, mumbling out the rest. "Everything is such a freaking mess."

"How about the beginning?" At her odd tone, I spread my fingers to peek through them before letting out a huff and dropping my arms. The jig was up. She was holding one of the many past due notices that had been on my table in her hands while giving me a pointed look. She waved the piece of paper in her hand and added, "You know, starting with the stuff you've clearly been keeping from me."

I let out a weary sigh, glaring at the big red letters at the top of the piece of paper she was holding, letters informing me if I didn't pay up soon, I'd be in deep shit—at least that was the gist of it. "Okay," I conceded. "But I'm going to need a *lot* of booze to get through this."

"On it," she declared like the incredible friend she was.

"God," Cheyanne said on a breath once I finished giving her the whole truth. "I know I've never met her, but I *really* hate your mom."

"*Pfft*. I wish I could hate her," I said, then hiccupped obnoxiously. "'Cause maybe then it wouldn't hurt so damn bad every time she lets me down." The margaritas had been strong tonight, thanks to Cheyanne's heavy pour, and as I lifted the straw to my lips to finish off my third, slurping the last of it down obnoxiously loud, I was seriously feeling the effects. Considering what a lightweight my best friend was, I was surprised she wasn't passed out on the living room floor already.

"Hey, why aren't you wasted right now?" I asked accusingly, squeezing one eye closed to make the two Cheyannes in front of me less bleary.

"Because I've been adding an extra shot of tequila to each of your drinks to keep your tongue loose."

I pointed a wobbly finger between both her faces, unsure which was the real one and which was the tricky trickster. "You clever little minx. You trix-ed me . . . tricked-ed-ded . . . tricked me. Ha! Got it on the first try." I congratulated myself by attempting a pat on the back and wobbled on the couch before righting myself.

Cheyanne snorted, giving her head a shake. "Yeah, sure

you did, drunky. Now get your shit together and stop changing the subject. I'm really upset with you right now."

My buzz went from hardcore to sluggish as her words penetrated the haze of alcohol. *Damn it*, and for a millisecond there, I almost forgot my life was about to be flushed right down the shitter.

"I know," I said on a heavy sigh. "I'm really sorry."

She sat beside me, taking the empty glass I was currently trying to suck every last tiny bit of margarita out of and set it on the coffee table in front of us. "Babe, why didn't you tell me? We're best friends, we're like family. You're Auntie Lu-Lu to my daughter, for crying out loud."

I covered my face, the guilt gnawing at my insides until I started to feel hollow. She'd sat there for more than an hour now, silently listening as I laid out every gory detail of the last few ugly months, the whole time the pain in her eyes growing starker. "I know," I replied on a painful groan. "And I've hated keeping all of this from you. It's been eating away at me for months."

"Then why did you? I could have helped. You could have worked for me," she exclaimed, saying exactly what I knew she'd say. "I would have loved to work with you, day in and day out." Her top lip curled up in disgust. "At least then you wouldn't have had to work in that disgusting pit."

I tilted my head to rest it on her shoulder, feeling the slightest bit lighter. "I love you, you know that, babe, and I know you wouldn't hesitate to help, but I feel like I need to do this on my own. I know that sounds ridiculous given the state of . . . well, my dumpster fire of a life right now, but it's just how I feel, you know?" I sat up tall and shifted to face her full on. "Kind of like, I got myself into this mess, and I have to find a way to get myself out of it. Whether that's the smart choice or not, I don't know. It's just what I have to do."

She looked like she wanted to fight, like she wanted to smack me across the back of the head until I saw reason. But that wasn't the kind of friend she was. She was the kind of friend who supported the people she loved, even if she didn't agree with them.

"All right." Her tone indicated she was relenting under duress. "I'll let you do this. But"—she jabbed her finger in my face to emphasize her point—"I'm going to have your back every step of the way. No more secrets. Understand?"

"Got it," I promised.

"*And*," she stressed, expanding on her concession, "if you're at risk of losing anything, *anything*, I expect you to let me help you. Understand? I won't compromise on that."

Honestly, I would have expected nothing less. When Cheyanne loved someone, there wasn't anything she wouldn't do for them. Sure, our relationship had changed a bit since she met and fell in love with her gorgeous, über badass fiancé, Trent Montgomery, but that was what happened when you met the person you wanted to build a life with. Still, she always made sure to make time for me and to let me know she was there if or when I ever needed her. Truth was, I counted myself lucky to be among those Cheyanne kept close to her heart. I couldn't have asked for a better friend in all the world.

"All right, deal." However, I had a concession of my own. I snatched my glass up and shoved it at her. "But only if you pour me another drink."

Four

NATE

M y headache had grown steadily worse throughout the day and the constant tap-tap-tapping of my passenger's shoe against my dashboard wasn't helping.

That's all I'd heard for the past eight, nearly nine hours, that fucking tap-tap-tapping. Well, that and her snarky comments and bitchy attitude when she forgot she was supposed to be giving me the silent treatment.

I let out a sigh of relief when the sign for Whitecap came into view, knowing this nightmare of a car ride was nearly over. We'd finally made it to the small beach-side town in Oregon where I'd grown up, the very same one I'd left so many years earlier because I was convinced I was meant for more.

The irony was that I'd come back for the very same reasons I'd left in the first damn place. Used to be, I couldn't stand how damn small this place was, how everyone knew everyone, how secrets didn't exist in a place like this, and that gossiping about everything was practically the religion for most of the townsfolk. I'd felt like I was suffocating, growing up here. Hell, half the time I got in trouble for stupid shit wasn't because my parents caught me, but because someone *else* had seen me acting like a dumb kid and reported right back to my folks. My friends and I hadn't been able to get away with a damn thing. I was counting on that still being the case.

Back then, the one thought that had been at the forefront of my mind for most of my life was how I couldn't wait until I was old enough to get the hell out of Whitecap, and the moment I could, I made good on that promise to myself.

To my parents' dismay, the only colleges I applied to were the ones that took me out of state, the same for law school as well. Then, instead of coming home upon graduation like they'd hoped, I took an internship at a prestigious firm in San Francisco that eventually turned into a full-time job.

For the past twenty years, northern California had been my home, and I'd been happy there. Well, maybe not happy, *exactly*, after all, a marriage that felt more like a prison sentence followed years later by a contentious divorce tended to put a damper on pretty much everything. But at the very least, I'd been content because I had Evan. Then everything changed.

"For the love of God, will you knock it the hell off? That damn tapping is about to drive me insane." I took one hand off the steering wheel so I could pinch the bridge of my nose, my headache growing to the point I could feel my heartbeat behind my eyeballs. "And get your feet off my dash, already. I won't tell you again."

Evan's response was to grumble and mutter under her breath in that surly teenage girl way that had evolved into an art over the centuries. At least she took her damn feet down, but not before scuffing the hell out of the dashboard in the process.

Whoever said parenthood was a blessing either hadn't experienced what it was like attempting to raise a teenager, or they were simply full of shit. My vote was on the latter, personally. It seemed like Evan's sole reason for existing was to push my buttons and tell me on a daily basis all the creative ways I was ruining her life, of which there were a ton apparently.

To be fair, she wasn't making my life all that easy either. I swear, the instant she turned fourteen the sweet little angel I met and fell ass-over-elbows in love with twelve years earlier when she was just a little doe-eyed toddler was taken over by some kind of pod person. Overnight she became a moody, sullen version of herself who hated everything and everyone and didn't hesitate to say so.

I flipped on my blinker and made a left, suddenly swamped with memories as the Boardwalk Inn came into view.

To say Evan had taken the news of our impending move badly was a laughable understatement. The entire evening before my trip had been filled with yelling and tears and threats of running away. It had been so bad I'd considered nailing her windows shut before I left the next morning.

Because of the drama that had unfolded beforehand, when I'd made this very same trip from San Francisco to Whitecap a month ago, I hadn't exactly been in the best of moods. I'd come back to my hometown to get everything in order for this move. I'd spent three days with a real estate agent, looking for somewhere to set up my office, somewhere I could make a home for Evan and me. Office space had been easy enough since I wasn't all that picky, but I hadn't managed to find a single house I thought a bratty, emotionally turbulent teenager would like, so I'd settled on a two bedroom apartment in the middle of town.

I'd turned into the parking lot of that dive bar because it was the first place I'd noticed outside Whitecap's town limits that served alcohol, and after the belligerent voicemail I'd just gotten from my daughter, I'd needed a drink more than my next fucking breath. Stumbling upon the redheaded stunner working behind the bar had been an unexpected silver lining to an otherwise miserable trip.

There hadn't been a single day in the past month that I hadn't thought about our night together, and every time it happened, I found myself fighting a hard-on like some pathetic teenager instead of a forty-year-old man who was supposed to have more self-control.

To say that had been the best sex of my life would have been putting it mildly. I was pretty sure I'd had an out of body experience every time I came that night. Which made it a crying shame it was only a one-time deal. She'd made that perfectly clear when she refused to give me her name and bailed out of my hotel room before the sun had even risen. Not that I was complaining. With the move and trying to get a new business off the ground and a kid who was a hop, skip, and jump from a juvenile detention center, the last thing I had the time or inclination for was a romantic entanglement. The fact the woman lived one town over and I'd more than likely never see her again was icing on the cake, really: a pleasant memory amidst months of unpleasantness and worry.

On autopilot, knowing these roads like the back of my hand, even after so many years, I made another turn onto the main drag through the center of town. Evan sat up a little higher and leaned forward to get a better view through the windshield, pulling me from my ill-timed thoughts of a certain redhead. "Wait . . . where are we?" she asked, her voice holding the smallest tinge of panic, and I knew exactly why.

"Welcome to downtown Whitecap," I said, the shit-eating grin I fought to keep from my face ringing clear as day in my tone.

"Oh my God," she said with a dramatic whine as she threw herself back into the seat. "Are you kidding me right now?"

That was her new favorite thing to say. *Are you kidding me right now* was the question that followed anything she didn't like, and nowadays, the list of shit my daughter didn't like was ungodly long.

"Nope, not kidding you."

"This place is a joke! I haven't seen a single Starbucks in like, *forever.*"

I pointed through the windshield to the long row of shops and storefronts that stretched across the whole block on my left. The once-red brick was now bleached, thanks to the sun and salty breeze, and housed the Whitecap Bank, the ice cream shop that stayed open year-round, no matter how frigid the winter months were, and a few other businesses. And right there, in the middle of it all, hung a shingle that read "*Welcome to Drip. Come on in and stay a while.*"

Don't mind if I do, I thought as I turned the wheel and guided my car into one of the diagonal spots that faced the large plate glass windows on the face of the building. "You don't need a Starbucks when you can support your local businesses. That's the kind of stuff small towns thrive on."

Back in the day, this spot had housed a popular deli. The owner at the time, Burt Macklan, had always talked about retiring to Florida where it stayed warm year-round but still had plenty of beaches. I guess he finally made good on that plan. Now it was a coffee shop that seemed to be doing pretty damn good business for midday during a work week, at least from what I could see beneath the flare of the sunlight on the sparkling clean glass.

"Let's go," I said as I pushed the button to kill the ignition and unclipped my seatbelt. Our new home was less than ten minutes away. My parents' general store—our destination before heading to the apartment complex—was at the end of the block. But if I didn't get some caffeine in my system to help beat back this headache and improve my sour mood, I was liable to explode, and the aftermath wouldn't be pretty.

"I bet their coffee sucks," she grumbled as she burrowed deeper into the passenger seat and crossed her arms over her chest with an indolent pout. "I'm not going in there."

"That wasn't a request. Now, quit your sulking and get out of the car."

Evan's eyes rolled so far back in her head it was pure luck they didn't get stuck staring at the inside of her skull. "Oh my God, you're *literally* ruining my life," she decreed dramatically. That was her second favorite thing to say lately, how I was *literally* ruining her life.

"Do your old man a favor, and crack a dictionary, kiddo. Look up what the word 'literally' actually means."

She curled her top lip up in a sneer. "*Ugh*, how old are you? No one owns dictionaries anymore. You look it up online."

Was forty too young to have a stroke? Not if it was stress induced, right? "Then google what it means. But do it once you're out of the car."

"Jeez! What's your deal? I'm fourteen, not a little baby. I can stay in the car by myself for a few minutes."

A bark of laughter erupted from my throat. "Now who's kidding who here?" Pulling my aviator style sunglasses off, I tossed them into a cupholder and twisted in my seat to face my girl—the light of my life, even when she was driving me to insanity—full on. Bracing my forearm on the steering wheel, I rounded my eyes in bewilderment. "It's not lost on you why we're making the move here in the first place, right?"

"Uh, because you want to make my life miserable?" she sniped sarcastically. "Yeah, I kind of got that."

I pulled in a calming breath, counting down from ten before I dared respond. "No. We're here because of you and the terrible decisions you were making."

She threw her arms up, flailing in the seat. "I told you a million times, that whole thing with Kelsey's mom's car was an accident!"

That *thing* with the car she was so casually referring to was that while she and a few other girls were staying overnight at their friend Kelsey's house, they decided there was absolutely nothing wrong with taking Kelsey's mom's car out for a little 3:00 AM joy ride. Only Kelsey had been sucking on a vape pen all damn night that contained more than just nicotine and ended up crashing the fucking thing into a light pole because she was high as a kite. It was a goddamn wonder none of them had been seriously hurt, and that middle of the night call from the police station had shaved a good ten years off the end of my life. I'd had plans for those years, thank you very much, and now they were just gone, replaced with even more gray hairs.

And as catastrophic as that had been, it was only the tip of the iceberg. She'd gone from a straight A student, regularly on the honor roll, to failing nearly every class.

She'd stopped spending time with the friends she'd had since kindergarten and started hanging out with a whole new crew that did shit like get high and steal their own mother's car, for Christ's sake. She backtalked, she threw attitude. If she decided not to skip school—something she'd started doing with alarming frequency—she was getting in trouble with teachers and the principal for being insubordinate. She'd even started dressing differently, her clothes mainly consisting of varying shades of black and gray, all of which had tears in them I wasn't convinced were put there by the designer. She bounced between two pairs of shoes, a beat-up pair of Chuck Taylors or black combat boots. She'd even started doing her makeup differently, wearing black eyeliner rimmed so thick you could barely see her beautiful eyes. When I'd put my foot down and refused to let her dye her hair black, you'd have thought I told her I was packing her up and shipping her off to a convent for the fit she threw.

But the straw that broke the camel's back was when I came home early to pick up some documents I'd forgotten in my home office, and found a half-dressed nineteen-year-old shithead trying to climb out of her bedroom window. The only reason I hadn't called the cops on him was because it was obvious he'd been lied to. I'd never seen a human being faint before, but that was exactly what he did after I informed him she was only four-*fucking*-teen. Eyes rolled back in his head, skin turned white as a sheet, and he passed the hell out, hanging halfway out a second story window. Broke a couple bones on the fall, for good measure.

Evan's mom had written her off months before as being a problem child beyond saving, choosing instead to give full custody to me and pretend she didn't exist under the guise of tough love. Her last words in regard to her own daughter was that Evan shouldn't bother to call until she got her act straight. I'd wanted to ring her goddamn neck, and might have actually done it if it hadn't meant Evan would lose the only stable person she had in her life to prison time.

I refused to give up on her, however. I'd tried every-thing I could think of to pull her out of this downward spiral: I'd grounded her, I'd taken away her phone and tele-vision, I'd enrolled us in counseling—together and sepa-rately—but nothing worked. It was as if she'd erected a wall around herself, and I couldn't get through. I couldn't scale it and get to the girl I loved trapped behind it. But I wasn't going to stop trying, damn it. She wasn't something you could just write off, she was a person, she was *mine*, and if my parents had taught me anything, it was that you never *ever*, gave up on the people you loved. And Evan had my whole entire heart. So I'd climb and climb until my fingers bled, never giving up hope I'd scale that damn wall.

This move was my latest attempt at making things better. I hoped that getting her out of the big city and away from the so-called friends she'd started hanging with would help her turn a corner. Only time would tell.

"You know what? The fact that you'd even try to defend yourself after that whole mess just goes to show how immature and irresponsible you are," I chastised. "So, no, you obviously aren't old enough to wait in a car by yourself. Now move it."

She grumbled and bitched the whole time it took her to get out of the car. Finally, after moving slower than any living human could possibly move, she slammed the door and stomped up onto the sidewalk. "There. Happy now?" she snapped.

Not even close, but I was only seconds away from coffee and just starting this new beginning I'd mapped out for both of us. So, while I might not have been happy in that very moment, at least I was hopeful.

As in: *Dear Christ, I hope like hell this works.*

Five

NATE

I'D SPENT SO LONG in San Francisco I'd forgotten what it was like to walk into a small-town establishment and have everyone stop what they were doing to look up and stare at the newcomer. That was one of those things I'd wanted so desperately to get away from back in the day, and as Evan and I entered the coffee shop aptly named Drip, my skin prickling with awareness at all the eyes pinned firmly on my daughter and me, I could say without hesitation I still wasn't a fan.

"Why are they all staring?" Evan whispered out of the corner of her mouth as we made our way up to the counter.

"Welcome to small-town living," I answered. "It's what they do." Pushing the feeling of being under a microscope aside, I inhaled deeply. The scent of freshly ground coffee beans that hit me the moment I pulled the door open was an instant jolt to my system. I wasn't sure there was a better smell on earth, at least not at that moment.

"See? This place isn't so bad. Kind of cool, actually."

Drip had embraced the whole beach town vibe but not in a tacky, over-the-top way. The walls were a pale mint green like sea foam, the trim and molding a soft blue that reminded me of floating in the ocean on my back and staring at the cloudless blue sky. The décor was also a subtle testament to the town with little anchor and lighthouse figurines and white macrame on the walls designed to look like old fishing nets.

The wall behind the counter was made to look like old, whitewashed shiplap with the menu written on a chalkboard in big, loopy script that was surprisingly easy to read. There were small bistro tables, two chairs to every table, lining the huge windows that looked out over the street, a long counter that looked to be handcrafted with repurposed wood to give the space even more character, and a display case at the end with pastries that looked so damn good my stomach flipped.

"If you like cheap décor that looks like they picked it up off the set of *Golden Girls*," Evan mumbled as she stepped past me without so much as a thank you for holding the door for her. "I bet they don't even serve oat milk here."

I shot her a bewildered look. "What the hell is oat milk?"

She looked at me like I was the world's biggest idiot. "It's exactly what it sounds like. Milk made from oats."

I didn't know how something like that was possible, but let it slide. "Well, if it's a real thing, I bet they have it here. And don't be a brat. I personally think this place looks nice." We moved up to the counter, and I lifted my head to read the menu above the serving window.

"Welcome to the Drip. What can I get—No way! Nate Warren? Is that you?"

At the sound of my name, I pulled my eyes from the boards to the woman standing across the counter from me. She had long, dark hair, magnolia pale skin, and big blue eyes. It was obvious she was younger than I was, but given the size of a town like Whitecap, that didn't mean much. Whether you were in the same class or not, you tended to know everyone.

It took a few seconds for recognition to dawn, but once it did, my eyes went round. "Monica Lamb?"

"Yeah," she said with a smile that would do toothpaste commercials proud. "Well, Monica Killborne, now," she corrected, holding up her left hand to reveal a rock big enough to ice skate on, resting on her ring finger.

That sparked a memory of my parents telling me years back that little Monica had gone off and married herself a retired NFL player. "That's right. My folks told me about that. I know I'm years late and all, but congratulations just the same."

She beamed as if she were still a newlywed. "Thanks. Georgia and Dezzy said you were coming back. I didn't realize they meant now."

"Things happened fast. In fact, we're on our way to the general store right after this. Just had to stop off for a caffeine boost after that drive." I placed my arm over Evan's shoulders, ignoring her annoyed *ugh* and attempt to shake me off. "Mon, this is my daughter, Evan. Evan, this is an old friend of mine, Monica."

"Not his *real* daughter," Evan said with a sneer, causing Monica's eyes to go wide.

It was the same argument we'd been having for the better part of a year. It didn't matter that I was the only father figure she'd had since she was two years old, or that I'd made it official and adopted her when she was five, shortly after marrying her mother. It didn't matter that she'd had my last name for nearly a decade. The moment my divorce to her mom was finalized, I'd become nothing more than *Nate* to her. It was almost as if she got off on telling everyone she came across she wasn't my *real* daughter, and I was getting really tired of being looked at like I was a kidnapper or pervert or something.

I tightened my arm around her shoulders so it was more of a headlock than a fatherly embrace. "Whether you like it or not, the adoption papers say otherwise."

Monica shook off her surprise and gave my daughter a friendly smile. "Well, welcome to Whitecap. We're excited to have you. You're going to love it here."

Evan crossed her arms over her chest and snorted. "I *seriously* doubt that."

"Enough," I clipped at her before dropping my arms and looking to Monica. "Sorry about that. You know how it is with teenagers."

Monica's smile was fading so fast it could have had its own dimmer switch, not that I could blame her. Evan had a gift for making things awkward with a capital A and didn't hesitate to pull out that talent whenever it suited her. And it suited her all the time.

"Well, then, this round's on the house for the newest Whitecap residents," she offered kindly, but I got the distinct impression she was trying to move us along to get us out of here . . . again, not that I blamed her. "What can I get you guys?"

"Just a large coffee. Black. Thanks."

Evan looked at her and arched a snarky brow. "Please tell me this place has oat milk."

For the love of Christ.

Luna

I pushed through the door of Drip at the tail end of the afternoon rush, that lull that hits about 3:00 when you need a boost to get you through the rest of the day. I'd timed it that way intentionally so Monica wouldn't be slammed when I came in.

Sure enough, the place was practically empty, with the exception of two or three customers who'd already been taken care of, and the second that bell tinkled like musical chimes her head came up and her eyes narrowed, nothing else to focus her attention on but me. Standing tall from where she'd been leaned over, counting receipts, she braced her hands on her hips and spat, "I was wondering when you were going to show your face."

My mouth pulled into a cringe. "I guess you talked to Cheyanne already?"

"You damn well know I did. That's why it's taken you three days to come in here and see me after confessing the truth to her, because you knew she'd filled me in and thought I'd be mad."

I pointed at her pinched face. "And you *are* mad, so I had every right to worry!"

"Damn right, I'm mad," she cried, smacking her hand down on the countertop. "You're one of my closest friends and you didn't feel like you could come to me?"

"I wanted to fix my own mess," I stated pathetically as I hefted myself up on one of the round, vinyl covered stools in front of the counter.

"I get that, and that's not why I'm mad. I'm mad because being there for someone you care about isn't all about solving their problems for them. At the very least, I could have just listened as you got everything off your chest. I could have been a shoulder for you to lean on. But you didn't give me that chance."

God, I really did have the very best friends a woman could possibly have. They were the family I got to choose after being stuck with one who was less than ideal, to put it mildly.

"I'm sorry. Looking back on it, I wish I'd come to you and Chey sooner. I know I should have, and I regret that. All I can do is say I'm sorry and I'll try to do better the next time my world is falling apart."

The hard, drawn line of her mouth wavered as one corner trembled with a smile she was trying desperately to hide. Finally losing her battle, she cracked a full grin at the same time she rolled her eyes. "All right, fine, drama queen.

I'm not mad anymore. After that apology, I actually feel bad enough for you to make you a coffee on the house."

I did a little jig right there on my stool and giggled. "Yes! Then my plan worked. I figured if I'm pathetic enough, I can start getting stuff for free. Tell me if you think this face will work on the people at the electric company." I made an exaggerated hang-dog face and batted my eyes.

She pulled back in a cringe and laughed, "Dear God. Do yourself a favor and don't make that face in public ever." I snorted as she started my regular order, a nonfat caramel latte with an extra shot. "Besides, you shouldn't feel special right now," she said as steam shot from the machine before it started whipping the milk into a creamy, feather-light froth. "Yours isn't the first coffee I've given away today."

"What, are you trying to go out of business?" I teased. "You can join the club I started. I'm the president, but you can be my VP."

She snickered and slid my steaming drink in front of me. "Georgia and Dezzy's son and granddaughter showed up here earlier."

My eyes went big. The news of the Warren's prodigal son returning after years had been the talk of the town for weeks now. Not only because Whitecap didn't get new residents all that often—mostly just those on vacation during tourist season—but because everyone in town loved the Warrens and were over the moon at how excited they were for their only child's return. The fact he came with his own offspring was just icing on the cake.

"Wow, really? That's big. I'm surprised this is the first I'm hearing about it. I bet Georgia and Dezzy are beside themselves. I don't know two people more fit to be grandparents."

"Yeah, well, I wish them all the luck in the world," Monica said in a way that made my chin jerk back in befuddlement.

"You say that like it's a bad thing."

"She's a teenager." Monica shrugged casually. "At least I hope that's the reason for her acting like a spoiled little brat while she was here."

My eyes bugged and I nearly spit out the sip of coffee I'd just taken. "Are you serious?"

She shook her head ominously. "Wish I wasn't. Nate's been gone a really long time, so I'm not a hundred percent sure how he turned out, but the grandkid, let's just say the apple fell pretty far from the tree."

Bracing my elbows on the counter, I cupped my chin in my palms, eager for a taste of the town gossip. "What happened?"

Even though the coffee shop was empty, Monica's gaze darted around cautiously before she leaned forward and lowered her voice, just to be safe. "Well, from what I gathered, the move was most definitely not her choice, because she was already fit to be tied when they got in here, and it was obvious the two weren't exactly getting along. Anyway, she waltzed in like she owned the place with this sour look on her face, and the first words out of her mouth was how the décor looked cheap and like it came off the set of *Golden Girls*."

I sucked in an offended gasp. "No, she didn't!"

"Oh, honey, she absolutely did."

Now pissed off on my friend's behalf, I smacked my hand down on the counter. "Okay, first of all, the décor here is *awesome*."

"I know!"

"Secondly, do *not* diss the *Golden Girls*."

Monica nodded. "That was exactly what I thought when she said that."

"I can't believe she actually had the nerve to say that to you, and that he didn't stop her."

"Well, in his defense, I'm pretty sure he didn't realize I heard her. She'd tried to mutter it, but she wasn't as quiet as she thought she was. Then, she was all up in arms about wanting oat milk in her coffee. When I told her I was out and only had almond, you'd have thought it was the end of the damn world. She ended up saying she didn't want anything, and I think Nate was feeling the embarrassment then. He just got a black coffee, shoved a ten in the tip jar, then dragged her out of the door."

My jaw dropped. "Wow. That's just . . . *wow*."

"Right? It'll definitely be interesting to see how things play out."

She could say that again.

Six

LUNA

"Georgia, I can't tell you how much I appreciate this," I said as I pulled the trigger on the price gun and slapped the sticker on the tube of sour cream and onion Pringles. "Thank you so much for bringing me on."

Georgia waved me off from where she sat behind the register, one of the romance novels she kept tucked beneath the counter open in her lap, her thumb holding her place. "You kidding? It's what we do in Whitecap. We look after our own."

I looked across the top of the short racks that made up the aisles and caught Cheyanne smirking, her expression screaming *I told you so*. I stuck my tongue out at her and went back to pricing chips.

In her version of letting me handle this whole business

on my own, she'd been pushing me to reach out to Georgia and Desmond Warren, the owners of Warren's General Store, for the past couple weeks, insisting they wouldn't hesitate to take me on. She could be so damn annoying when she was right.

Aside from Cheyanne's smugness, it was a pretty sweet gig. Georgia and Dezzy were incredible, I got to work with my best friend from time to time, and the biggest silver lining, working here meant I got to quit my job at the bar. Sure, I didn't make tips at the general store, but the pay was better and I didn't have to deal with creepy drunks leering at me in ways that made me want to scrub my whole body with bleach and a steel wool pad.

"Still," I continued, turning my attention from Cheyanne, "it means a lot."

"Of course, sweetie. Anything we can do to help. You know, Dezzy and I were just beside ourselves with worry when you told us your situation. We only wish we could do more."

"This is more than enough, really. But I love you both for caring so much."

They really were two of the best people I'd ever met. There wasn't a single person in this town who didn't love Dezzy and Georgia Warren. That love and adoration was why, even after her pottery business had blown up, Cheyanne still worked part-time at the general store. They were the closest thing she'd had to parents since she lost her own when she was six years old. They hadn't batted an eye at taking her on when she first showed up, out of nowhere and heavily pregnant, several years back. It was love and adoration from everyone in this town that kept the store going strong, even during those couple times a big box store tried encroaching on their territory. We were loyal here in Whitecap.

"You know, I'm not sure if I've told you this or not, but my son's recently moved back home." She had told me. Several times. As a matter of fact, she'd told everyone who passed through those doors. It was more effective than taking out a half page ad in the local paper, which I'm sure she would have done if she'd thought of it. To say she and Dezzy were excited that their only child had moved back after being gone practically half his life was an understatement if there ever was one. "He was a bigshot lawyer back in San Francisco." Something else I was well aware of, thanks to her. "Now he's setting up shop here in town, and he was just telling me the other day how he's in dire need of an assistant. Someone hard-working and trustworthy." She arched a brow at me. "Think I might know someone just like that."

The pricing gun in my hand froze halfway to the bag of sea salt and vinegar chips I'd been about to label. "Wait —seriously?"

"Well, yeah. I mean, if you think that's something you'd be interested in. I'd be happy to put in a good word for you."

Hell yeah, it was something I'd be interested in. A job like that was sure to pay enough to help me climb out of this hole I'd dug myself. There was just one issue. "I appreciate that, Georgia, but I just started here. I couldn't leave you in a lurch like that."

She blew out a raspberry and waved me off. "Child, please. If that's your only reason for not taking a shot at a fancy office job, go ahead and get that outta your mind this minute. Dezzy and I love having you as part of the Warren General Store, and you're welcome to stick around for as long as you want. But if something better comes along, I'd be disappointed if you didn't jump at the chance. You deserve wonderful things, Luna. Don't settle just because you're worried about us."

"She's right," Cheyanne added, nodding enthusiastically over the top of the shelves. "You should totally go for it. You'd be great at it. You have the perfect personality for something like that."

I pulled my bottom lip between my teeth and bit down. "You think so?"

"For sure. You're obsessed with calendar apps, you collect journals and notebooks the way little boys collect baseball cards, and you're borderline obsessive when it comes to organization."

"I'm not obsessive," I defended on a frown, throwing a snack-sized bag of Cheetos at her head. "I just think things should be where they belong. What's so wrong with that?"

"Not a thing, honey," Georgia assured me. "You don't listen to a word she has to say. You just do you."

"Thank you." I pointed at Georgia and shot Cheyanne a sneer. "See? She doesn't think there's anything wrong with me."

"Not at all," my new boss confirmed. "But now that you mention it, that stock room's really gotten away from us lately. It's a disaster. Maybe when you're done pricing you could tootle on back there and set things to rights."

I narrowed my eyes, slamming my hands down on my hips. "Oh, okay. I see how it is. You actually do agree with her." I pointed an accusing finger at a laughing Cheyanne. "You were just buttering me up so I'd do the work you hate."

"We all have our strengths, dear," she stated with an easy shrug. "Yours is organization. Mine's manipulation."

"Unbelievable," I griped, throwing my arms up.

"That's life," Georgia lamented. "Now, chop, chop little onion. That stock room isn't gonna organize itself."

Man, she was lucky I loved her.

Nate

I let out a tired gust of air as I turned into my parents' drive, exhaustion beating down on my body with the same strength the Hulk pounded his enemy into the ground. Evan and I had only been in Whitecap for a week and a half, but it had been the most exhausting week and a half of my life.

Not only was I trying to get my business off the ground, but because Evan had decided to get back at me for the move by sneaking out of the house a few nights before we were set to leave San Francisco and sending the cops I'd called to help me find my runaway daughter on a wild goose chase, she was grounded for the foreseeable future. And that meant I'd had to bring her into the office with me when it wasn't school hours so I could keep an eye on her.

To say the atmosphere between us had been tense lately was like calling Antarctica a little chilly. Things were downright hostile between us. So far, this hairbrained idea of moving back here to improve things between my daughter and me had failed spectacularly. Trying to wake her up and get her out the door for school each morning had been tougher than all three years of law school combined. When she was talking to me, which wasn't often, she was whining and crying about how bored she was in this town or how miserable her life was, or what a lousy father I was. It was a wonder I'd managed to get anything done at all the past several days. As it was, with her all but chained to my hip during the hours she wasn't at school, I was several days behind where I'd wanted to be. I should have had an assistant in place and been taking on clients by now, but *no*.

"Do me a favor," I said as I shut off the engine and turned to look at my sulking daughter in the passenger seat. "Don't act like a dick tonight. You want to be mad at me for enforcing the punishment your actions brought on, go for it, but your grandparents haven't done anything to warrant you acting like a brat under their roof, and I won't tolerate you treating them poorly. You think your life is miserable now? You don't want to see what happens when I have to get creative."

She rolled her eyes and let out a beleaguered harrumph. "Whatever, Nate."

"No, not whatever," I said, placing my hand on her arm to stop her when she reached for the door handle. I let the whole *Nate* thing slide, because that was a battle I chose to leave for another day, but I wouldn't let the *whatever* stand. "Confirm you understand what I just said."

"Jeez, all right! I got it. I'll *be on my best behavior*," she said in a deep mocking voice I could only assume was meant to be me. "Can we go inside now, or do you want to stay in the car all night long like a weirdo?" I waved her out of the car with one last sigh before climbing out of my own side.

The front door flew open before we made it onto the porch, my mother's face stretched into the biggest beaming smile at the sight of us. "Oh, you're here!"

She looked so damn happy to have us over for dinner, a dinner she'd cooked herself, more than likely slaving over the stove to make sure it was perfect after having worked at the store for hours. I was slammed with the same punch of guilt I'd been feeling since moving back. I really had been a shitty son the past twenty years—if not longer. That something as simple as a Sunday dinner put her in such a grand mood spoke volumes about how selfish I'd been. If the time spanning between my visits to see them had been months as opposed to years, it might have felt more natural. Now, a quick dinner was cause for celebration in her eyes, even though she'd seen us a few times already since we got to town.

"I thought I heard your car pull up, but I wasn't sure."

"Nate had to give me a lecture on behaving before he'd let me come in, like I'm a toddler or something," Evan informed my mom before blowing an obnoxious bubble with the gum in her mouth and letting it pop loudly.

My mother blinked at Evan's proclamation before dismissing it. "Well, now that that's out of the way, dinner is nearly ready. I only have a few finishing touches left. Evan, would you like to help me in the kitchen?"

She shrugged and popped that damn gum again. "Yeah, sure. Whatever."

I opened my mouth to get on her again—for all the good it would do me—only to have my mom place a hand on my arm to silence me. "Good, then," she spoke before I had a chance. "Go inside and wash up. I'll be in right behind you."

Following my mother's lead, I stayed quiet until the front door snicked shut. As soon as it did, she turned on me. "I see she's still doing the whole 'Nate' thing. I take it that means there hasn't been much improvement since the last time we spoke."

I couldn't remember a time when I'd felt more beaten down and exhausted as I felt just then. Expelling a weary breath, I lifted my hands and scrubbed at my face. "You'd be taking that correctly. There hasn't been a single pleasant word to pass between us since we got to town. The only time we aren't arguing is when we're asleep."

She narrowed her eyes in contemplation before humming. "Hmm."

"What? What's that hum supposed to mean? That's the hum you use when you think I'm doing something wrong."

"I don't know what you're talking about," she said with an innocence that didn't match the canniness in her eyes.

"Bullsh—" I stopped the curse before it could pass my lips, remembering how my mother hated it when I used foul language. Since I was under her roof—or close enough—I'd respect her rules, but if she'd been at my house, I'd let it fly without feeling bad. "You know exactly what I'm talking about. Just say it, would you?"

"All right, fine." With her hands on her hips, she hit me with the hard, stern Mom look she'd perfected throughout my life. "Have you stopped to think maybe all you do is argue because the only time you speak to her is to get onto her about this or that or to lecture her about what she's doing wrong? Have you once stopped to consider you're feeding off each other? Maybe instead of jumping down her throat, you should ask her how her day was first."

"What's the point in that?" I asked flatly. "I know how her days are because she spends them at school or chained to my side since she's not responsible enough to be left alone." The smack my mother laid upside my head left my scalp stinging. "Ouch, damn it! What was that for?"

"If you're the kind of stupid that can't be helped, that's one thing, but don't intentionally be obtuse."

"Jesus. Okay," I muttered as I rubbed at the back of my head. "I got it." I huffed out a breath. "And you're right. I'm failing her at every turn. I've been a pretty sh—crappy dad lately."

My mother reached out and took my hand, giving it an affectionate squeeze. "Parenting is the hardest job a person could ever have. Being responsible for another human being, trying to make sure you do what's best for them, it's enough to do your head in. No one on earth is perfect at it. You show me a parent who says they've done everything right and I'll show you a bald-faced liar. We make mistakes, all of us. All you can do is keep loving her, keep trying to guide her down the right path, and keep teaching her right from wrong. And be the bad guy who enforces punishment when she screws up." She gave my hand another squeeze. "But that doesn't mean it has to be a *constant* punishment. You just have to remember the little girl you love is still in there under all those hormones and teenage angst and drama."

"Yeah? I don't know about that." I gave her an arched look. "I'm pretty sure she's been taken over by some supernatural force, like a demon or alien or something."

She laughed, long and hard, like that was the funniest

damn thing she'd ever heard in her life. "Uh-huh. And just wait until she starts dating."

"Why the hell would you say something like that to me?" I shouted as she turned and headed into the house, leaving me all by myself after dropping that bombshell. "That was just unnecessarily mean," I grumbled as I followed the sound of her laughter inside.

Seven

NATE

"HEY, son. Hope you're hungry. Your mom's been at in the kitchen for hours." Dad was kicked back in a recliner, the footrest lifted and the back slightly lowered for maximum comfort, his eyes directed at the TV, engrossed in the game taking place on the screen.

"Hey, Dad." I looked over at the TV screen, my brow furrowing in confusion. "Wait. Are you watching soccer?"

"Sure am. Those boys have stamina I can't even fathom, running all over that field the way they do." He let out a whistle and shook his head. "Makes me tired just watching them."

"When the hell did you get into soccer. You know baseball season's already started, right?"

He popped a handful of sunflower seeds—his go-to

snack food when he was watching a game—into his mouth. "I know, I've got that recording to watch later. No commercials." He looked over at me like he was the cleverest son of a bitch in the universe, having discovered how to *finally* use that feature on his television after all these years. "But your mom made me watch this show with her a while back. *Ted Lasso* or something like that. Anyway, it's all about soccer, and I kind of got into it, so here we are."

I sat down on the sofa across from him with a chuckle. "Only you would get into soccer because of a TV show."

He lifted his finger into the air. "A damn good TV show. Want a beer?"

"Sure."

He reached down and flipped the lid open on the cooler beside his chair, tossing me one of the beers from inside. That cooler was another game day staple. Desmond Warren was serious about his sports. When he was in spectator mode, the only time his ass came out of that chair was to use the bathroom or replenish his snacks if he was running low.

I popped the tab on the can and brought it to my lips, taking a nice, long pull before letting out a deep sigh.

"I know that sigh," my dad said. "That's the sigh of a parent with a teenager. Quite familiar with that sigh myself. Matter of fact, I think I'm the one who taught you how to do it."

"Was I ever this difficult?" I asked, then thought better of it and raised my hand to stop him. "You know what, don't answer that."

Dad let out a chuckle and took a pull from his own beer. "Don't need to. Pretty sure you know the answer to that one already."

I drained nearly half my beer in a couple gulps. "Then I owe you and Mom the world's biggest apology."

He waved that off with an easy, "Meh. It's how everything stays balanced. Asshole kid grows up to have kids of his own who just so happens to also be assholes, because all kids are, and can suddenly relate to his parents. It'll all come full circle with Evan when she's an adult. You just have to bide your time, then the real fun begins."

"Oh yeah? What fun would that be?"

He looked over at me and winked. "The fun where you get to throw it back in her face and make her feel guilty for all the hell she put you through when she was an asshole kid."

"What you're saying is I have another ten to fifteen years before I see any kind of pay out."

He tipped his can my way in silent salute. "Hey, no one said this was an easy job. Worth it? Every damn day. Unless your kid's Dahmer or Bundy or something. But then the parents were most likely part of the problem with those two." Finally, he circled back around to what we were originally talking about. "Anyway, what I'm saying is it's tough, but worth it."

"I'll have to take your word on that."

The commercial break ended and the game resumed. We sat in silence for a few minutes, just watching the guys run back and forth across the field, working a tiny little ball in ways I hadn't thought humanly possible before my mother's shouted voice carried into the living room, breaking our concentration. "Dinner's just about ready! Get your behinds up and set the table."

That was a hard and fast rule in Georgia Warren's house and had been since before I was born. She never had an issue with slaving over a hot stove, spending hours in the kitchen whipping up delicious, creative meals . . . as long as that was where her work stopped. If we wanted to eat her cooking, it was up to Dad and me to make sure the table was set and the kitchen was scrubbed clean afterward. A fair trade in the eyes of anyone who'd ever eaten my mother's cooking.

We didn't dawdle at moving our asses, and by the time everything was ready to come out, the table was set, complete with full water glasses. The delectable smells and the familiar behavior transported me back to growing up under this roof, the dinners spent around this very table night after night. We never ate in front of the television or in separate rooms. Dinner was family time in the Warren household, a time for us share with each other the good and bad of our days. As I thought back, I was hit with that damn pang of guilt again, the one that came more and more frequently since my return to Whitecap.

I remembered how I hadn't appreciated the hour or so every evening spent with my parents, how jealous I was of my friends whose folks let them eat dinner in front of the TV or in their bedrooms. Back then, I believed I had a million other better things I could have been doing than hanging with my lame parents and telling them why my algebra teacher, Mr. Walter, was a certified dick.

As I pulled out the same chair I'd sat in for the first eighteen years of my life and lowered myself into the seat, I thought of how I would give anything to go back, even if it was just for one night, and do it again. Do it *right*.

"Smells divine, sweetheart," Dad said to Mom from across the table. "Just like always."

"You have Evan to praise as well," Mom decreed as she took her linen napkin and shook it out before placing it in her lap. "She mashed the potatoes nice and smooth. Seasoned them up too, all by herself."

I looked up from the bowl of potatoes in question I'd been scooping onto my plate. Across the table, my daughter's head was bent toward her lap, but I could see the tiny grin she was fighting.

I shoved the spoon back into the bowl and heaped out another scoop. "Then I'm getting extra," I declared as I plopped more potatoes onto my plate. "If they taste half as good as they look, I'm in for a real treat."

Evan's head shot up, her eyes widening as they met mine from across the table. "Really?"

That tiny bit of praise turned the heat up on my girl's cheeks, giving them a warm, pink flush, and she looked so surprised she could have been knocked over with a feather, and it hurt like hell. My mom was right. Just because things were rough going lately didn't mean it *all* had to be bad. I could make the conscious effort to do something besides yell and scold.

"Absolutely, baby girl. I think you might have even topped your grandma in best mashed potatoes."

That flush grew even deeper and her smile widened as she scooped green beans onto her plate.

Maybe, just maybe, everything would work out after all, I thought as I dove into my meal with more gusto than normal, especially when it came to the mashed potatoes. I was actually starting to feel hopeful that Evan and I were close to turning a corner.

I should have known better than to think we were in

the clear, because things went right back to how they'd been roughly halfway through dinner.

We were talking about our days, like we'd done my whole life growing up, and the conversation turned to my law practice. "Word through the grapevine is that you still haven't found an assistant yet."

I looked over at my mother as I chewed the bite I'd just taken and swallowed. "How in the world is something as boring as that considered grapevine worthy? Is there nothing better to gossip about in this town?"

Mom simply shrugged. "Not quite yet. You two are still the newest arrivals." She paused and pointed her fork Evan's way. "Well, *she* is. You're the mysterious boy who left, only to come back years later as a dashing man."

Evan made a retching sound and followed it up with a dramatic. "Oh, *gag*."

My mother carried on like she hadn't said anything while I cut my girl an evil glare that made her giggle. Just the sound of it was enough to warm me from the inside out. "Anyway, if you're still in need of an assistant, I think I've found you the perfect one."

Oh hell.

Before I could interject, she was off like a rocket. "She's smart and efficient; I know this for fact because she's working at the general store right now."

My dad looked up, finally seeming to cotton onto the

conversation taking place around him. "You talking about Luna?"

Mom nodded. "Sure am. She's got a great head for organization, and she caught our books up in no time flat."

There had to be a catch. There was *always* a catch. "If she's so great, why would you risk losing her to me?"

"Oh, I'd be happy as a clam if she'd stay on with us forever, but a woman like that's meant for bigger and better things. As much as I love the store, as proud of it as I am, and I am proud, don't you get me wrong, a woman like Luna is meant for something more. And I'm telling you the God's honest truth, you won't find yourself a better assistant in all the world."

"She's not wrong about that," Dad said in solemn agreement.

"It's just icing on the cake the woman's got the kind of looks that'll knock a man flat on his rear end."

Well shit, there was the catch.

"Not to mention, she's smart, funny, and has a heart bigger than the whole state of Oregon."

"Not wrong about that either," Dad interjected again.

"Come on, guys. Don't start."

"What?" Mom gave me a look dripping with innocence that was as big a lie as my ex-wife's blonde hair. "I'm not starting anything. I'm just telling you about your new assistant is all. What you choose to do with that information is strictly up to you. That said, any man who doesn't fall over their tongue for Luna Copeland is either blind or just plain stupid."

"For Christ's sake," I grunted, reaching up to pinch the bridge of my nose. "I'll interview her for the job, but that's it," I added quickly and firmly when it looked like she was about to expire with joy. "*Only* the job, you understand?"

"Whatever you say," she said with a grin, thinking she was sly.

"I'm serious, Mom. Dating is the furthest thing from my mind right now." However, that didn't mean I wasn't fantasizing about a certain nameless redhead so often my dick and my palm had gotten extremely acquainted with each other over the past several weeks. But that wasn't about a relationship. That had just been sex. Fucking *incredible* sex.

But until things with Evan were on more solid ground, splitting my attention between her and someone else wasn't an option. When I'd filed for divorce two years ago, it hadn't been with any sort of idea of remaining a bachelor for the long haul. That relationship might not have worked out, but that didn't mean I wasn't willing to try again, truth was, I didn't mind the thought of another committed relationship. I'd even started thinking of putting myself back out there, maybe try my hand at a couple dating apps. But when things with Evan started rolling downhill at lightning speed, the thought of dating left my mind completely.

"Now that that's settled, who feels like some dessert? We've got homemade apple cobbler and vanilla bean ice cream."

"That sounds great. Evan loves apple pie, so that's right up her alley."

"I don't eat sugar."

My head whipped in her direction, my eyes growing wide. The smiling, relatively happy girl who had been sitting across from me all through dinner was gone, in her place, the sullen, broody kid I'd been dealing with for the better part of a year. "Since when?"

"Since forever," she exaggerated. "You'd know that if you paid any attention. God!" With that, she whipped her napkin down on the table and shoved back in her chair so hard the legs scraped across the floor loud enough to make me wince.

"Where are you going?" I asked in bewilderment at the sudden and unexpected mood change.

"To the bathroom, if that's all right with you," she shouted as she stormed out of the dining room. A second later the bathroom door slammed.

"What the hell just happened?" I asked more to myself than anyone else.

"Ah, teenagers," Mom lamented. "I don't miss that age, I tell you."

"Well, that was interesting," Dad observed casually. "Now how about that dessert?"

Eight

LUNA

STRESS EATING HAD BEEN A VERY real thing in recent months, and the navy pencil skirt I'd chosen for my interview was tighter than I remembered it being. It still worked, just barely, and hadn't quite reached obscene. The creamy silk blouse in the palest baby blue stretched tighter across my breasts than it had before. Fortunately, it had a bow neckline, the tails draping down to cover my chest that had grown more ample over the past few months thanks to Little Debbie and her sisters, Hostess and Mrs. Baird.

The outfit was one of the few leftovers from my old life, the one in which I ran my own business and had stylish, classy outfits to wear to client meetings and such. Now I had to pray the seams didn't bust when I sat down during my interview for a job as someone else's assistant.

When things had been particularly bad money-wise, I'd taken most all my other frilly duds and designer heels to a local consignment shop. The owner, a sweet woman in her mid-fifties, had taken the whole lot off my hands, whether she felt she had the clientele for it or not, and had done her best to push my wares on her customers. Thanks to her, I'd been able to keep my A/C going during an unseasonably hot month.

I'd taken the time to blow my hair out so it was as smooth and shiny as the undisturbed surface of a lake. I kept my makeup subtle, lighter than I usually wore it. Just a few swipes of mascara to bring out my eyes, a soft pink blusher on the apples of my cheeks with just a hint of shimmer, and a tinted gloss to give my lips a rosy hue. It had been so damn long since I had a job interview, I felt like a fish out of water. Nerves fluttered around in my belly like a whole swarm of butterflies jacked up on Mountain Dew.

I closed my eyes and pulled in a long, steadying breath before looking at my reflection in the mirror. "You can do this," I said, hoping to amp myself up before the interview. "You're a hard worker, you're a fast learner, and this guy'd be lucky to have you."

My pep-talk was cut short when my cellphone rang, startling a yelp out of me. "Jeez, Lu, get your shit together. It's just a phone, for God's sake."

Cheyanne's face popped up on my screen when I accepted the FaceTime call. "Oh, good. I was worried I'd miss you. I wanted to wish you good luck on your interview."

My cheeks puffed out on an exaggerated breath that turned into a loud, obnoxious raspberry, and that was all it took for my best friend to read my mood.

"Uh-oh. What's wrong?"

"I'm nervous as hell is what's wrong. I haven't had a job interview in years. What if I suck and he shoots me down?"

"He won't," she insisted.

"You don't know that. And all my business-y clothes are too tight. Things are going to be pretty dicey if I have to sit down."

Cheyanne curled her lips between her teeth to keep from laughing. "I'm sure it's not that bad."

"Oh yeah?" I hit the little button on my screen to flip it around so she could see my whole body in the mirror I was standing in front of. I twisted this way and that so she could get a look at me from every angle.

"Okay, I might see your point," she said on a snort. "The skirt's a little snug, but it still works. You'll just have to be careful, is all. Or hey! Maybe you can borrow something of mine," she offered.

"I appreciate that, babe. Just two problems. First: we

aren't anywhere near the same size, even before my stress binge added some additional poundage to my ass. Second: even if I could wear your clothes, there's no time for me to get to you and change." I turned to look at the alarm clock sitting on my bedside table. "Actually, I need to get going, or I'll be late."

"All right, hon. Good luck. You're going to do great, and he's going to hire you on the spot."

I could only hope.

Only a few blocks from the heart of downtown Whitecap, Warren Law Firm sat in a tidy little two-story house with board and batten siding painted a soft yellow, crisp white trim, and windows so spotlessly clean they shimmered like crystals in the sunlight. Like all the other houses on this street, it had been converted into a business sometime in the late eighties. To the left of the firm was a hair and nail salon and dentist's office. A few buildings down on the right was the daycare Cheyanne's daughter, Renee, frequented. There was also a therapist's office, a bakery, and an accounting firm all along the same road.

The anxiety that had been churning in my belly gave way as I started up the walkway. The tiny postage stamp yard, remaining from the building's days as a home, was surrounded on three sides by the most adorable picket fence and covered in a thick blanket of deep, vibrant emerald green grass with a small bed of brightly colored petunias and an azalea bush near the front entrance.

I felt I was being welcomed by the adorable entryway, like the flowers and everything else were inviting me in. For the first time since I'd started getting ready, I actually felt good about this interview.

"I've got this," I mumbled under my breath as I reached for the handle of the glass door. "I'm fabulous. I'm going to blow this guy away, and he won't be able to hire me fast enough."

The door glided open on well-oiled hinges without so much as a squeak, and I stepped across the threshold onto the restored parquet wood floors. The place had gone through a massive gutting at some point, changing the entire layout of the first floor from what I could tell. To the left of the entryway was a huge open space that looked to be a waiting area. Two large brown sofas were pushed against the walls to form an L with an end table tucked into the corner of the wall where they met. A nice, relatively new lamp sat on that table, along with a stack of magazines that had been fanned out across the surface. A matching coffee table sat in the center of the seating area with a choice of newspapers to read, a decorative bowl of iridescent stones, and tapered pillar candles of different sizes.

At the very back of the large, open room was the kitchen, or what used to be the kitchen, at least, now set up as a breakroom with a small, round table and four chairs like you'd expect to see if most breakrooms or mall food courts. Off the right of the break area was a set of open stairs that led to the second level loft area. Against the far-right wall, between one door marked 'Restroom' and another with a name plate that read 'Nathanial Warren, Attorney at Law' was a long white desk, bare of anything but a flat silver computer monitor and a gray mesh ergonomic office chair. That had to be where the assistant would sit.

The whole place would have felt rather utilitarian had it not been for the sunlight streaming through the large, gridded windows on the opposite wall. It wasn't a bad view. Nothing particularly scenic, but a side view of the street stretching off into the distance. If I got the job, it would be nice to see people milling about, traveling up and down the sidewalks, during the day. *If* I got the job. Damn, I really hoped I got the job. I'd have been happy staring at a cinderblock wall all damn day if it meant I was working at that desk.

But in order for that to happen, I needed to actually interview first, which meant I needed to find the guy in charge. "Uh . . ." I cleared the croak out of my throat and tried again. "H-hello? Mr. Warren?"

"Sorry. Sorry," I heard a disembodied voice call from the loft area above. "Be right down."

I pasted a smile on my face so it would come through in my voice as I assured, "Oh, no worries. Take your time."

I moved toward the waiting area and paced a short distance, back and forth, back and forth, for a solid minute before a large figure started down the stairs. "I apologize for the delay," he said, his head lowered to the file folder open in his hands. "Things around here have been a bit chaotic."

As soon as Nathanial—or Nate, as Georgia had told me—rounded the base of the stairs and started in my direction, blood began to rush in my ears, muffling everything he was saying, because the man coming toward me, the one who'd yet to look up from the documents in his hands long enough to realize I was about to have a coronary right in the middle of his waiting area, was none other than the stranger from the bar all those weeks back. The very one who'd rocked my world so thoroughly, I'd felt him in every tiny twinge and pull between my thighs for three days after the fact.

This wasn't supposed to happen. I was never supposed to see that dude again. He was just a one-night stand who was supposed to go back to his part of the world and remain nothing more than a fond memory. He was defi- nitely *not* supposed to be the son of the two people I respected most in the whole wide world.

Son of a bitch!

Finally, when only a scant number of feet separated us, he looked up, those fog-colored eyes I remembered with perfect clarity widening at the sight of me. "It's you," he breathed, and I could have sworn one corner of his mouth trembled in a suppressed smile. "Wow. This is unexpected. Where did—I mean . . . This is crazy. How did you find me? You wouldn't let me give you my name or anything."

And for damn good reason! I thought to myself. Because this was precisely the situation I tried so desper- ately to avoid whenever I picked a man to have a casual, no-strings fling—or in Nate's case, a one-night stand —with.

Closing my eyes, I reached up and massaged at my temples, trying to fight off the headache pulsing behind my eyeballs. "This can't be happening," I mumbled to myself. The smell of leather and cloves suddenly filled my senses, a smell I hadn't been able to forget for *weeks*. A smell that made my knees weak and my core throb. A smell that was strong enough it could only mean he'd moved closer when I wasn't paying attention. My eyelids popped open. Sure enough, he'd closed even more of that distance between us. "You aren't supposed to be here," I said accusingly. "I specifically asked if you were a local, and you said no."

"You never asked me that."

I let out a sarcastic laugh. "Oh, I absolutely did!" I knew that because it was the same thing I asked any and every man who caught my attention , because hooking up with a local was a huge, screaming N.O.

"No. You didn't. I remember clearly, you asked: 'Are you from here?'"

"*Exactly!*"

He arched a condescending brow as he continued. "And seeing as we were in a different town, I answered correctly. No, I wasn't from *that* town. I'm from this one. Or, well, I was. Growing up. And I guess again, since I moved back."

"From San Francisco," I said, filling in the blanks in my mind, tiny little puzzle pieces suddenly clicking into place.

"That's right. How did you—?" He broke off, realization finally dawning. "No," he said on a long, drawn-out breath.

"Yep."

"You're Luna Copeland?"

"And you're Nate. Georgia and Dezzy's son." *Well, that's just freaking perfect*, I lamented silently.

He dropped one arm to his side, causing the stiff green

file folder to smack against the side of his thigh as he raked his other hand through that thick, sandy hair that couldn't decide if it wanted to be dark blond or light brown. It was the kind of hair that, given any time in the sun, would streak light all on its own.

"Jesus God," he grunted as he moved to drop the folder on the desk that would—fingers crossed—soon be mine. "This is a fucking mess."

I let out a small, uncertain laugh. "Yeah, well, it'll definitely make working together a little awkward at first, but we're both adults, right?"

The look on his face was one you'd expect to see if you'd suddenly sprouted a third eye out of the middle of your forehead or something. "Oh, that's not going to happen."

I rocked back on my affordable yet stylish heels that I'd picked up at Target a couple towns over. "What? Why not?"

He lifted his hands in a placating gesture. "I'm sorry, really, but I don't think this is going to work."

This couldn't be happening. I wasn't sure what I'd done to Karma in this life or a past one to piss her off so tremendously, but the vindictive bitch clearly had it out for me. My cheeks and neck heated with anger as my hands balled into fists at my side. "So, that's it? You're not even going to let me interview?"

"Look, I only agreed to the interview as a favor to my mom. It was never a guarantee." *Asshole*, I thought bitterly. "I took a look at your résumé, and you aren't exactly qualified. I mean, the last job you had was at that dive bar one town over."

"Incorrect," I seethed. "My last and *current* job is at Warren's General Store. Obviously you didn't look at my résumé close enough, or you would have seen that." Okay, so maybe it wasn't the strongest argument, but I was floundering, without a life raft in sight. I hadn't realized until that very moment that I'd gotten my hopes up about this job. I needed it more than I was willing to admit to anyone, even myself.

"Well, work history aside, it's pretty clear this situation would never work out."

"Because we banged each other stupid for *one night*?" I asked incredulously, my voice rising higher with each word. "Are you kidding me?"

He went from cool and breezy to hard and caustic in a flash. "I've always considered it to be a good business practice not to dip one's pen in the company ink, so to speak. And considering I know exactly what you feel like wrapped around my dick, I'd say we already crossed that bridge and burned it to the ground. You may not agree, but seeing as this is *my* business, my say is the only one that really matters. I'm sorry you wasted your time coming in here."

I threw my head back with a sardonic "Oh my God. Were you this big of an egotistical asshole when we first met, or is it a new thing? Because there's no way in hell I would have slept with you had I seen this side beforehand. Gotta say, Nate, it's rather unattractive."

He crossed his arms over his chest and scowled. "Too late to take it back now, sweetheart. That night already happened."

"Oh, believe me, if I could go back in time and undo every choice I made that night, I absolutely would. And not only because it cost me a job, but because your lackluster performance is so not worth the regret."

The smirk he gave me just then told me he was aware I was lying my ass off. It was so arrogant, so self-satisfied, that I wanted to slap it right off his perfectly chiseled, unfairly handsome face. "Yeah? The scratch marks you left on my back and the noise complaint I got the following morning don't really say lackluster to me."

I had to get out of there before my anger exploded and my skull did an impression of a boiling tea kettle with steam coming out of my ears. Full of indignation, I whipped around on my heel only to jerk to a stop when I saw the girl hovering in the doorway.

"Hi," I squeaked, unaware that we'd had a lurker, especially one who appeared so young. It was harder to gage her actual age, what with the raccoon thick eyeliner she had rimming her eyes, but her skin was still dewy, free of any lines or blemishes. The long, lanky legs, encased in shredded fishnets and denim shorts and attached to somewhat rounded hips spoke to a girl's body developing into a woman's, so she had to be in her pre or early teens. Which meant I hoped to hell she hadn't overheard anything that had just been said. I couldn't imagine the kind if long lasting psychological damage it could do to a kid to hear about her father's sex life, I didn't want any hand in the years of therapy that would might require.

Her eyes—I thought they might be blue, but it was hard to tell with that heavy-handed makeup—darted over my shoulder to the man behind me, disregarding me all together. "I thought I heard yelling when I was walking up." Well, it seemed she'd missed the sex talk, at least. Thank God for small miracles.

"It's nothing you need to worry about, kiddo. How was school?"

"It was school," she answered with all the enthusiasm of a dead fish that had been rotting on the beach for at least a week. She gave me another glance, an incredulous once-over. "Who's she?"

I opened my mouth to introduce myself, only to be rudely interrupted. "This is Luna Copeland, the woman your grandmother recommended I interview. Luna, this is my daughter, Evan."

"Not his *real* daughter," she established.

"For Christ's sake. Not this again," Nate grunted, pinching the bridge of his nose. "An adopted daughter is just as real as a biological daughter."

The girl shrugged. "Whatever."

Deciding to ignore the parent/child squabble building in front of my very eyes, I took a step closer and held out my hand. "Hi, Evan. It's nice to meet you."

She looked at my hand, then back to my face, hers a blank canvas that gave absolutely nothing away. "I got homework." With that decree, she hooked her thumbs through the straps of the backpack on her shoulders and moved right past me like I wasn't even standing there. She did the same to Nate, grabbing an apple from the bowl on the counter of the break area before trundling up the stairs on heavy, combat boot-clad feet.

"She's a real ray of sunshine," I deadpanned.

Nate let out a sigh I'd heard from Cheyanne more than once when Renee was being less than the perfect angel she was ninety-nine point nine percent of the time and was pushing her mommy's nerves. The very sigh that had miraculously disappeared the moment her man Trent came into her and Renee's life and gladly took on half the load. It was the sigh of an overwhelmed and exhausted single parent. It was also not my damn problem. Not after he'd been such an overwhelming dickbag.

"I'm told it's a phase," he said in a tone that was equally conversational and exhausted. "But I'm not so sure about that."

"Yeah, well, good luck with that," I snarked. "Also, go to hell."

I whipped around, determined to hold my shit together until I got out of there. And as soon as I locked myself in my car, I gripped the steering wheel with white knuckles, threw my head back, and screamed my frustration into the void until I went hoarse.

Nine

LUNA

AFTER MY NEAR-PSYCHOTIC meltdown in my car outside the Law Firm of Dickbag and Douchenozzle—witnessed by only three or four passersby, I'd managed to drive myself home where I proceeded to burst into a fit of ugly, snotty sobs—you know, the kind that make your face splotch so it looks like you have hives? Yeah, those.

Anyway, I was about to pour myself a bottle of wine when I decided it probably wasn't the healthiest outlet, so I did the next best thing. While Cheyanne made some of the prettiest, most creative pottery I'd ever seen, and Monica made the best cup of coffee on the West Coast, my talent lay within my green thumb.

Needing the peace and tranquility I received from tending my gardens and the numerous beds spread across my property, I stomped up the stairs to my room and changed into a pair of yoga shorts and a racerback tank. Being a natural redhead, I slathered on my SPF before I headed outside and, coupled with my floppy, wide-brimmed gardening hat, I was safe from those evil rays.

No one who knew me would dare to call me a romantic. All my friends knew I avoided commitment like it was covered with massive, festering boils and pox. But despite that, I had a serious weakness for romance novels that stemmed all the way back to my childhood. Like death and taxes, it was guaranteed that Madeline Copeland would bounce from one boyfriend to another like a rubber ball, and it wasn't exactly rare that she'd tie herself to a man who skeeved me out in a serious way.

When that happened, I'd spend as much time as possible at the local library to avoid going home. I'd sit in one of those hard wooden chairs for so long, pouring over stories, my butt would eventually go numb, but I'd loved every second. It wasn't just an escape from my mom's latest handsy, pervy boyfriend, but from reality all together, and it was *exactly* what I needed.

It was there that I cultivated my love of fiction. I started with things like Matilda and Sideways Stories from Wayside School. As I got older, I shifted to all the Fear Street books by R.L. Stine. Then one day, a day like any old day, it happened. I was browsing the stacks for my latest adventure when I saw a cover, out of place from all the books around it—I found out later it had been mis-shelved by accident—that grabbed my attention and refused to let go. On it, a man dressed as a pirate from historical times—his long, unbound hair whipping in the breeze, his shirt inexplicably undone to reveal ripples of muscles—was holding a peasant woman tightly around the waist as her boobs heaved from a partially untied bodice.

I'd snatched that book up, holding it to my chest like a dirty little secret, and found somewhere tucked away to dive into a world of sexy marauding pirates and the tavern wenches they'd kidnap, forcing them onto the violent seas during a dangerous voyage where they'd eventually fall madly in love and bang like rabbits from port to port. The pirates gave way to rakish dukes and other sorts of nobility, then once I'd poured through all those, I'd stumbled on the more modern billionaires, cowboys, celebrities, professional athletes, and men in any type of uniform you could dream up. The similarity in all of them was the romance and the happily ever after.

If my friends had any idea that their self-professed life-time bachelorette was a sucker for sappy love stories, I'd never live it down. I'd harbored that secret for longer than any other I could remember, eventually shifting to audio-books when they became a big thing. Now I could stream to my heart's content with the click of a button.

With my latest novel unfolding in my ears, I got to

work on the flowerbeds bordering my front porch, ripping out weeds and clipping off dead flowers like a mad woman, tossing the spent blooms in a basket at my side. In no time at all, the stress of the day started to melt from my shoulders beneath the bright, warm sun heating my skin. There wasn't much that could keep me down when I had my hands buried in the cool, rich earth. It was easy to keep my mind off the bad when I was doing something I loved.

I was in the zone, so focused on my book and my task at hand that the tap on my shoulder scared the ever-loving hell out of me. With a battle cry that probably sounded more like a cat being drowned, I whipped around, falling on my ass in the middle of my begonias. "Back the hell off," I shouted as I flung my gardening shears wide in self-defense. In hindsight, it probably would have been smarter to keep them in hand while defending myself, but I hadn't exactly been thinking straight at that moment.

"Whoa! Jeez, crazy," Cheyanne cried, raising her hands in the air and taking a step back. "It's just me!"

I pulled out my earbuds and stuffed them into my pocket. "Oh my God, Chey." Sucking in a deep breath, I placed my hand over my heart to keep it from beating out of my chest. "You scared the crap out of me. What were you thinking, sneaking up on me like that? I could have seriously hurt you."

She let out a snort as her brows creeped higher on her

forehead. "Seriously? Your aim was about five feet wide, and I was standing *directly* behind you. Pretty sure I was safe."

I blew out a raspberry and rolled my eyes. "Well, I coulda hit you if I wanted to," I said on a pout.

"Momma, look!" Cheyanne's daughter popped out from behind her and pointed at me. "Lu-Lu's butt smooshed all her flowers."

"That's right, shorty. My butt smooshed my pretty flowers, and it's all your mommy's fault."

Renee tilted her head back to her mom with an expression that dripped with disapproval. "That was mean, Mommy."

"Yeah, Mommy," I said on an exaggerated pout, poking my bottom lip out and everything.

"Okay, okay. I'm sorry I made you squish your flowers with your fat butt." I stuck my tongue out at her but took her offered hand and let her help me up. Renee skipped around my front yard, doing cartwheels and singing about my fat butt. I was going to make Cheyanne pay for that.

"But seriously, I'm sorry for scaring you. I thought you heard us pull up."

"I was listening to music." The lie rolled off my tongue easy enough, and I didn't feel the least bit bad about it, especially not after the fat butt joke. "I didn't hear you, sorry." Dusting off the back of my shorts, I sent a forlorn look to the begonias that were definitely going to need replacing before turning back to my friend. "What brings you and my shorty by?"

"I wanted to see how the interview went. I know I could have called, but Renee's been missing her Lu-Lu, so I figured, two birds with one stone and all that jazz."

I let out a huff, the anger I'd been feeling earlier giving way to defeat and disappointment. Crossing my ankles, I lowered myself back to the ground, mindful of my plants this time. "Let's just say, it could have gone a lot better."

Cheyanne pulled up a patch of grass beside me, crossing her legs in front of her, and together, we looked out at Renee dancing around the yard and brandishing a dead twig like a magical wand.

"You would have been so perfect for that job," she insisted. "What happened?"

I pulled my bottom lip between my teeth and bit down as I tried to figure out how to explain the situation I was in. "Well . . . you see . . ." I hemmed and hawed as my brain spun like a top. "The thing is. No—what had happened was—"

"For the love of God. It's obvious there's a story here. Just spit it out already."

"I kind of slept with him a while back."

Her head jerked around so fast it was a wonder she didn't give herself whiplash. Her eyes went big as she stared at me silently. She blinked, then blinked again before finally speaking. "How is that possible? He's been here less than a month. And you don't hook up with locals."

All facts. However . . . "It was back before he moved here, I guess. I'm not exactly sure of all the details. He came into the bar while I was working—"

"Wait, you mean that hole-in-the-wall place you were at before Warren's?"

"Yep. That one. Anyway, he came in, looking all kinds of beat down. He didn't exactly belong in a place like that, so it was pretty hard to miss him. We got to talking, he made me laugh, and when I asked if he was from here, he said no. He thought I was asking about the town next to Whitecap where the bar was. It was a huge misunderstanding. He had a room here at the Inn, and I ended up meeting him there after my shift ended."

"Okay," she dragged out, confusion pulling her brows down into a V.

"We didn't exchange names," I explained. "So I thought he was just some dude passing through. A one-time deal. Then I walked into that interview today, and lo and behold, the guy I'd banged six ways to Sunday is the lawyer running the place."

"That had to have been . . . awkward." It was obvious she was trying to hold back her laughter, but I didn't see what the hell she found so funny about any of it. It was a clusterfuck of epic proportions.

"That's putting it mildly," I deadpanned. "So, there I am, my mouth hanging open, and at first, he thinks I've somehow managed to track him down. He actually seemed excited about that." That realization made my belly flip in a way it had no business flipping. "Then he realized I'm the chick his mom referred for the assistant's job."

Cheyanne seemed to be hanging on to my every word, her eyes round and rapt on me, all she was missing was a bucket of popcorn. "What happened after that?"

"You mean after he informed me he made it a habit not to shit where he ate so I wouldn't be getting the job?"

She sucked in an indignant gasp. "He did *not* say that!"

"Well, not exactly that. What he actually said was he couldn't hire me because he knew what it felt like to have me wrapped around his dick." And what in the living hell was so wrong with me that I felt happy little twinges between my thighs as I recalled that?

"Wow," Cheyanne breathed, then blew her top. "That conceited, self-important pr—" She caught herself just as Renee came barreling up. "Momma! Watch my handstand! Are you watching? You gotta watch! You too, Lu-Lu. You both gotta watch me!"

"We're watching munchkin," I assured her. "Show us what you've got."

She darted away again and executed a handstand for all of half a second. "Did you see? Did you see?" she crowed. "I did it!"

"You did, baby. Good job." Cheyanne and I both clapped. "Now keep practicing."

"Aren't you worried she's going to break her neck?" I questioned as I watched Renee fall three times in the span of ten seconds.

"Nah. Kids her age practically have rubber bones. Now back to what we were talking about. What a prick," she finished on a whisper-yell so her kiddo wouldn't hear Mommy saying a bad word.

"Yeah, you're telling me. I have to say, five minutes in his company, and I can't for the life of me understand how two people as amazing as Georgia and Dezzy could have made someone as awful as him."

"Well . . ." She curled her shoulders toward her ears on a giggle. "Five minutes in his company while you two are dressed," she teased. "Because I think your first meeting went a lot better than this last one."

"You're terrible!" I cried on a laugh, picking a handful of grass and throwing it at her face. The blades caught on the salty breeze coming off the water behind my house and blew them away before they could get close to her.

Cheyanne giggled uncontrollably as she leaned away from the flying grass. "I'm not wrong, am I?" She arched a knowing brow, daring me to disagree. "After all, you never would have let the man anywhere near your pants if there hadn't been something there the first time you met."

"Yeah, well, now I regret the whole damn thing, and not only because I really needed that job." I stopped, the heaviness that had been resting on my shoulders for months, the same heaviness that had started to lighten when Georgia had first mentioned the position because I'd been stupid enough to hope, fell from the sky right onto my back, drooping my whole body beneath its weight. My voice came out small, quiet, and sad as I admitted, "I really wanted that job, Chey. It would have helped so much."

She hooked her arm around my shoulders and pulled me against her. "I know, honey," she said softly. "I know. But screw that guy, and screw that job. You don't need it."

But didn't I? Yeah, I really, *really* did. But I liked where her head was at. "Yeah. Screw him and his stupid job. I wouldn't want to work for a jackass like that anyway." Lie, lie, lie. But whatever.

"What's a jackass?" Renee asked loudly as she came dancing up to us, once more, twirling that stick wand of hers. In her eyes, she could probably see glittery swirls of magical light trailing behind it. Oh, to be a kid with that kind of imagination again. Life was so easy at that age. Well, for most kids anyway.

What had started as an *uh* turned into an *oof* when Cheyanne shoved her elbow into my ribs.

"Remember that talk we had about grownup words? You know, the words you're not supposed to repeat?"

"Oh yeah." Renee visibly perked up, grinning big. "Like when Daddy called that guy in the giant truck a motherfucker that one time."

I got another elbow to the ribs when I choked down a laugh that turned into a snort. "That's exactly right, sweetie."

Renee danced back off, hopping and skipping as she hummed out whatever tune was playing in her head. I might not have gotten the job, I might be in the same desperate situation I'd been in for months with no end in sight, but at least I had good people in my life. And without even trying, Cheyanne and her precious girl made everything just a little bit better.

Ten

NATE

TO MAKE MORE of an effort with Evan, I'd texted my mother earlier and asked for the recipe for her lemon butter and herb salmon. Then I'd thanked the good Lord above that Whitecap wasn't so small it didn't have Instacart and ordered everything I'd need to make a nice family dinner for my daughter and me.

Evan had darted upstairs and closed herself off in her bedroom the moment we got home from my office, so I'd poured myself a glass of wine, rolled the cuffs of my shirt up, and gotten to work on dinner. Long before I was old enough to leave home and start my own life, my mother had made sure I knew my way around a kitchen. To her thinking, there was no excuse for a human being to live off fast food and takeaway, and everyone should know how to make the basics, at the very least. Because of her teachings, I was on the lower end of the scale between being a passably decent cook and an award-winning chef. And if the smells coming from my kitchen were anything to judge by, I might have had a winner on my hands.

I plated the salmon on a bed of arugula that drizzled it with the lemon butter sauce, added the grilled asparagus and roasted new potatoes, then carried the plates to the table that separated the kitchen from the living room. It wasn't very big, but given the size of the apartment I'd rented until Evan and I could find something permanent, it was the only thing that would fit in the space. Same went for most of our furniture. We squeezed what we could into the apartment and put the rest into storage for the time being.

The place wasn't anything to write home about, but the complex was only a couple years old, so the fixtures and appliances were new, the carpets were still in good shape, and the paint was fresh. As an added bonus that it was centrally located between her school and my job. Lastly, there was the fact that, on a clear day—of which Whitecap had a fair few—you could stand out on the living room balcony and see the ocean in the distance. If the breeze was strong enough, you could smell the sea salt in the air and hear the cries of the gulls that were never far from the churning water.

"Evan," I called as I pulled open the silverware drawer and grabbed what we'd need.

"What?" she called back.

"Dinner's ready."

That declaration was met by silence for a few beats before I heard the sound of her bedroom door opening. A second later her head popped out over the second story railing. "What?"

"I said dinner's ready. Come on down."

She moved down the stairs at a snail's pace, never in a hurry to do much of anything unless it was her idea. The expression on her face was full of apprehension as she rounded the staircase and shuffled toward our little table. "What's going on here?"

I rolled my eyes at her. "Nothing. I just figured I'd make us dinner. Is that a problem?"

Her brows went up as she moved closer to inspect the food. "You cooked?"

"Yep."

"I didn't even know you *could* cook."

That statement slammed into me like a three-hundred-pound offensive tackle. The realization I'd been dropping the ball more than I'd originally thought was a humbling experience. The fact that my own daughter didn't know I could cook spoke volumes on how badly I'd been failing. I made a silent promise to the both of us right then and there that I was done putting in half measures. If I was going to piece my little ragtag family together again, I couldn't half-ass it. I needed to give it my all.

"Grandma taught me everything I know. By the time I was your age, I was making dinner for everyone a couple times a week."

"As like, punishment?"

I stopped on my way back to the fridge and cast her a bewildered look. "What? No. Not as punishment." I waved my hand at the chair I'd designated as hers. "Have a seat."

"Wait, so I have to eat in here? With you? Like, together?"

"Yes. Together, like a family, where we can tell each other about our days and partake in conversation like human beings. Sit." She huffed and rolled her eyes, probably cursing me in her head, but she eventually gave in and sat. "In regard to your earlier statement, I cooked dinner for my family because I liked it. I've always enjoyed cooking; it relaxes me. What do you want to drink? Water, iced tea, or soda?"

A cheeky expression took over her face. "How about a glass of that wine you've got opened on the counter."

My smile was full of sarcasm. "Try again, kid."

Her sigh was aggrieved. "Fine. Soda," she answered

disappointedly as she picked up her fork and started prodding at the fish and asparagus with little enthusiasm.

I grabbed a can of Coke for her and poured it into a glass, then topped off my wine before heading back to the table. She muttered her thanks when I set her drink in front of her, but I didn't miss the look she'd cast at my own glass. She was just asking for trouble, really.

Her tone came out slightly scathing as she asked, "So, if you like cooking so much, why didn't you ever do it before?"

I let out a sigh as I shook the cloth napkin out and placed it in my lap. "I wish I had a reasonable excuse for that. Fact is, I put work first, and that was a shitty thing to do. I made the excuse that I was too busy instead of moving things around to make the time, but I'm trying to fix that now."

She didn't exactly look convinced, but I took it as a good sign when she cut off a small corner of the salmon to sample.

"What do you think?" I asked as she chewed pensively. "I figured you could rate the meals and that would determine whether or not I added them to the regular lineup."

Her eyes went big. "Wait, so this is going to be a regular thing?"

Jesus, I really had done a shitty job as a parent lately. Even more than I'd originally thought. No wonder Evan had started acting out. "I'd like it to be. Look, sweetheart, I'm trying here. I don't want us to be at each other's throats constantly. Whether you believe it or not, I love you, more than anyone else. That's why I moved us here. This move wasn't a way to try and punish you."

She let out a snort and mumbled, "Could've fooled me. This town blows."

"Hey, watch your mouth," I scolded.

"Well it does," she insisted passionately. "I mean, there's nothing to do here. I don't have any friends because they're all back in San Francisco, so I don't have anyone to hang out with or talk to. It's totally lame."

"Those kids you hung with back in San Francisco weren't your friends. They were part of the problem. You can make new friends here." I hoped to Christ they were better than the ones she'd picked before.

"Easy for you to say," she muttered as she moved things around on her plate. "You're old. You don't get it."

I pointed my fork in her direction. "First off, forty isn't old. I'll have you know, I'm in the best shape of my life, thank you very much."

She curled her top lip. "Gross."

"Second," I continued, choosing to ignore the disgust on her face, "I understand more than you give me credit for. I left a life behind too. I don't have any friends in this town either, so I have to make new ones, just like you do."

"You mean like that woman from earlier today?" she asked snidely.

"What woman?" I asked in confusion.

She pinned me with a chilly glare. "You know, the one from your office. The redhead. She *is* your friend, right? I would think so, considering you guys slept together."

Fucking hell. I'd really hoped she hadn't heard that part of the argument earlier. I wasn't sure I'd ever be prepared for a conversation like this with my daughter, but as much as I wanted to sweep it under the rug, I knew doing so would only make things worse.

"That's . . . complicated."

"How?" Evan prodded. "You *did* sleep with that woman, right? That was what I heard you talking about, anyway. Which, by the way, yuck! I *really* didn't need to hear that. But still, if you slept with her, that obviously means you like her."

No way in hell was I about to explain to my fourteen-year-old kid what had transpired the night I'd met Luna. "Yeah, sure," I hedged, my brain desperately trying to come up with anything to get me out of this situation. "I mean, I like her fine." *For a woman I didn't know the first thing about*, I thought grimly.

"So are you two like, dating now?"

I nearly choked on the bite of fish I'd just taken. I lifted my glass and threw back more wine to clear my throat.

"What?" I wheezed. "Christ. No! No, of course not. I barely—I mean, that's just not—"

"Because you told Grandma you weren't dating right now."

"That's right. I'm not," I agreed quickly.

Jesus, was it hot in here? And why the hell did my shirt feel like it was too tight. I tugged at my collar, suddenly finding it hard to breathe. I had no clue how to navigate the minefield Evan had just shoved me into.

"Is she going to work for you?"

"Who?" I asked, using the back of my hand to wipe the beads of sweat off my forehead.

"The woman from your office today. She came in to interview, right? Are you going to hire her?"

"No."

"Why not? You said you guys were friends, right?" Her brows went up, her gaze shrewder than it should have been for a kid her age. "Because you slept together. And Grandma said she'd be perfect for the job. So why aren't you hiring her?"

"She just wasn't a good fit. That's all."

I could tell she didn't believe me by the look on her face, but I'd be damned if I said anything else. Picking up my fork, I shoved a bite into my mouth and chewed viciously. Thanks to our current topic of conversation, I couldn't tell if it was good or not, considering everything tasted like sand in my mouth. "If it's all right with you, I think I'd like to talk about something else."

"Whatever," she said with a shrug, and at that *whatever* I swore I felt a tick behind my temple and my eyelid started to twitch. "This whole family dinner was your idea. I'm just doing what you wanted."

Damn her. Damn her to hell for being too goddamn smart for her own good.

"Oh, and just so you know, I don't like fish."

Son of a bitch.

It was late, Evan was in bed for the night, and the sun had long since been swallowed by the ocean when I stepped out on the balcony with my cellphone and a cigar. The night was quiet enough for me to hear the swell of the waves crashing against the shore.

I stood at the railing and lit the cigar until the tip glowed a warm amber in the darkness. I puffed a few times, holding the smoke in my mouth before slowly blowing it out into the salt breeze.

I'd forgotten how peaceful the nights were in White-cap. Having lived in the city for so long, I'd gotten used to the constant noise, no matter the time of day. The quiet could have been disconcerting if I hadn't let myself embrace it.

I took another puff, forming my lips into an O to blow the smoke out in a perfect ring as I stared at the black-as-night water in the distance. The moon hung big and bright in the sky, the glow of it splattered across the tops of the moving waves, making it look like a painting that had come to life. I could have stood there for hours, easily losing myself to the rhythmic crash of the surf, unfortunately, that wasn't a luxury I had at the moment.

Knowing what needed to be done, despite how fucking much I dreaded it, I lifted my phone and scrolled through the numbers I had stored until I reached the one I'd been looking for.

With a resigned sigh, I hit go and lifted the phone to my ear as I took another puff from my cigar.

The call connected, and a moment later, my ex-wife's voice came through the line. "Nate?"

"Hey. I didn't wake you, did I?"

"No, it's fine. I'm just getting ready to head out in a few minutes."

Since I had yet to change out of my work clothes, I looked down at the watch still on my wrist with a frown. "Christ, Amber, it's nearly eleven on a Wednesday night. Where the hell could you be going so damn late?"

"What do you care?" she asked in a brittle, biting tone.

"It's none of your damn business anymore what I do with my life. We're divorced, *remember*?"

Oh, I remembered, I couldn't possibly forget. Because ending our marriage had been my idea, an idea she'd disagreed with passionately, she'd gone out of her way to make the whole goddamn thing as painful as possible, dragging the process out just to keep her claws in me as long as she could.

It shouldn't have come as a surprise when I told her I was moving out and filing for divorce. It wasn't as if either of us had been happy in our marriage for a long time. Truth was, I should have ended it years earlier, but I hadn't, for the same reason Amber was caught off guard when I finally called time of death. Because of Evan.

I stayed in that toxic relationship for as long as I had because I hadn't wanted to lose my daughter. Hell, if I was honest, Evan was the only reason I'd married Amber in the first damn place. That wasn't to say I hadn't loved my wife at one time, but my love for her daughter had been first, most, and instantaneous. The moment Amber had introduced me to that little girl with yards of tangled blonde hair and blue eyes too big for her face, I'd been a goner.

Amber's and my relationship probably would have fizzled long before ever getting to the altar had it not been for that little girl. She'd dug herself so deep under my skin, there was no getting her out. She became mine in every way that mattered. I knew the only way I could remain her father was if I made things official with Amber, so I had, then I'd turned right around and made Evan legally mine.

She'd been my daughter from the moment I met her, and despite of how rough the past year had been, I loved her as much today, if not more, than I'd loved her back then. She was the only human on the planet I'd step in front of a bullet for. Amber knew how much I loved our daughter, and she counted on that to be enough to keep me around, even though the love between us had fizzled to nothing years and years before I found the nerve to end it.

The divorce had taken a year to finalize, thanks to Amber jerking me around, fighting the custody agreement, and even going so far as to try and have my adoption of Evan overturned. It had been a tough year for my baby girl, but I told myself once it was all said and done, the three of us would find a way to work on building our new normal. Only, that hadn't been the case. For the past year after the divorce was finalized, Evan had started on this downward spiral that eventually ended with our move to Whitecap, but before that, her mom had all but washed her hands of her own flesh and blood, making an already bad situation that much worse.

I let out a sigh, closed my eyes, and pinched the bridge of my nose to tamp back my frustration. "Look, I didn't call to fight."

"Then why did you call?" she sniped.

Jesus, this woman. "I called because Evan's having a tough time, and I thought maybe it would help to hear from her mom."

Amber's tone came out cold and uncaring as she said, "I told you, until she gets her act together, I have nothing to say to her." It was just one of the shining examples of the woman she was, the woman I'd blinded myself to in the beginning of our relationship, all so I could keep Evan as a part of my life. Amber had always been apathetic toward her daughter, something that never sat well with me and had caused the bulk of our fights. Well, that and her jealousy. The woman was so narcissistic she couldn't stand it when she thought I paid more attention to our kid than to her.

If I could have reached through the phone right then and rung her neck, I gladly would have. "You ever stop to think that maybe part of her problem is her own mom doesn't seem to give two shits about her?"

"Of course," Amber snapped. "Blame me, just like always. Everything is *my* fault. Do *you* ever stop to think that maybe she wouldn't be acting out if you hadn't ripped our family apart?"

The laugh I let out was so bitter it burned my throat on the way up. "Oh, give me a fucking break. You couldn't give a damn about keeping our family together. The moment I agreed to the settlement your lawyer proposed, you were all too happy to sign on the dotted line. All you ever gave a shit about was money. It's why you fought the divorce as long as you did, holding out to see how much you could squeeze out of me."

"If I was so terrible, why the hell did you stay married to me as long as you did, huh?"

I stubbed the cigar out with more force than necessary as I ground out, "Don't ask stupid questions. You know the goddamn answer to that already."

"You *always* loved her more than me," she seethed through the line, sounding like a whiny, petulant child.

"Damn right. Because she's *my daughter*, and like it should be with every parent, my kid comes first, above all else. Obviously, that's a lesson you never learned." I shook my head in disappointment, my shoulders suddenly feeling heavy. "Christ, you are so fucking selfish."

Her voice had a razor-thin edge to it when she responded, her words cutting. "Then, by your way of thinking, if I'm such a terrible mom, Evan's better off without me."

"I didn't say that," I gritted, anger creating a red film over my eyes. "I never said that; don't put fucking words in my mouth." But I couldn't lie and say I wasn't thinking it. However, better off or not, Evan loved her mother, whether or not their relationship was healthy.

"You know what? I don't have time for this," Amber clipped into the phone. "I have plans, and they don't include another lecture from you. You wanted her so damn bad, now she's yours; handle it."

With that, she hung up, leaving me wondering for the millionth time how I'd ever managed to love someone who loved themselves above all else.

Eleven

LUNA

"I DON'T UNDERSTAND. It doesn't make any sense, I tell you. No sense at all."

I curled my lips between my teeth and gave big eyes to Cheyanne. We were both on shift at Warren's General Store today, and with no choice in the matter, I had to tell Georgia I hadn't gotten the job at her son's firm.

She'd been devastated, more than I could have expected and, for the last five minutes, had been saying the same thing over and over. She didn't understand. She didn't understand.

"I think, maybe I just wasn't the right fit," I explained, feeling the uncanny need to ease her distress. "It's really okay."

"No, it damn well isn't," she said, slapping her latest

125

romance novel down on the counter. "And not the right fit, my droopy round behind."

"Oh, Georgia, no. You don't look a day over thirty," Cheyanne said, trying to lighten the mood, and earned herself an angry-mom scowl for her efforts.

"Don't you try to sweet talk me into being in a better mood. I'm fit to be tied right now and I intend to stay that way. You would have been the *perfect* fit for him, I just know it. No sense, I tell you. This makes no damn sense. I have half a mind to call him and find out what the hell's wrong with his fool head."

A wave of panic crashed over me. Abandoning my task of restocking the beer in the refrigerators along the back wall, I ran toward the front of the store, chasing after Georgia as she made her way to the register where she kept her cellphone. Cheyanne matched me step for step, coming up the aisle beside mine.

"No, please, don't waste your time. Really, it's fine."

"Yeah, you don't want to go putting your nose in your son's business, right?" Cheyanne threw out, desperately trying to latch onto something that would save my ass. "I mean, how would you feel if he came in here telling you who you should and shouldn't hire?"

"Exactly!" I agreed swiftly.

Georgia didn't exactly pause in her mission, but she did slow down, thank God. "I get what you're saying, but the main difference between this and the scenario you pointed out is that I'm right."

"I'm sure he's under enough pressure as it is, what with the move and starting his own practice and being a single parent." And being a raging dick, I thought to myself. "You wouldn't want to add to that stress, would you?" I felt lower than low, playing her in such a way, but I respected this woman like crazy, and the last thing I wanted was for her to know I'd had a one-night stand with her only son, especially since my desire to stay single and untethered was already a bone of contention with her.

She stopped, and I nearly collapsed in relief. "Well," she dragged out. "That's true. He's had it pretty rough lately. I mean, first the divorce, then everything with poor Evan. What that child's gone through? No wonder she's acting out the way she is."

I had to admit, my curiosity was more than a little piqued by that, but I couldn't let it distract me.

"See? I know you want what's best for me, but I'm going to be fine. And it just means I get to spend more time here with you and Dez," I added brightly, hoping I wasn't going overboard.

Georgia cupped my cheek. The affectionate gesture made my vision swim, and I had to blink to keep the tears at bay. She was so tender, so loving, everything my own mother never was, and I'd have given anything to have had a mother like her. "I only want you to be happy, sweetheart. Happy and healthy and stress-free. You and Cheyanne are like my own babies. You're my girls. I want you both to have everything you could possibly want."

Oh man, could this woman get any more incredible?

Reaching up, I placed my hand on top of hers and gave it an affectionate squeeze before letting out an *oof* when Cheyanne barreled into me from behind and wrapped us both in a group hug.

"I love you both," she said with a sniffle. "You guys are the freaking best!"

My laugh was raspy with emotion. "I love you guys too," I said, wrapping one arm around Georgia at my front and the other around Cheyanne at my back.

The moment was unexpected and beautiful, but short-lived when the whimsical chime of the bell over the door alerted us to a new customer, forcing us to break apart.

"Sorry to interrupt, ladies, but I'm afraid we might have a problem."

I turned at the sound of the familiar voice. Sheriff Michaels, an extremely attractive man somewhere in his late-thirties to early-forties, stood in the opened doorway of Warren's General Store. It was obvious by the tan uniform shirt and olive-green tactical pants that he was on shift, but what I didn't understand was why he was standing there with his hand on the shoulder of Nate's teenaged daughter.

"Evan?" Georgia broke from our little huddle and started toward her granddaughter. "What in the world is going on?"

Sheriff Michaels kept his hand firmly on the girl's shoulder, pulling her back when she took a step toward Georgia. "You know this girl, Mrs. Warren?"

Georgia planted her hands on her hips and shot him a hard look. "I do. She's my granddaughter. Now, I've known you since you were born, Sheriff. I had a hand in catching you when you used to strip your diaper off and run around naked every chance you got, so you better tell me what's happening before I'm forced to call your mother."

For a big, strong man in authority, he sure did blush fast under the haranguing of a sweet old lady.

"Yes ma'am," he muttered before remembering he was the sheriff of these here parts and pulling his act together. It was all so funny I looked back over my shoulder at Cheyanne so we could share an inconspicuous giggle. At least until he spoke next. "I just so happened to be driving by on my way back to the station when I caught this one out front, keying a black Chevy sedan. A Malibu, I think."

A record scratched in my head as I whipped back around. "Wait. That's my car." My feet started moving before I could form a thought, carrying me out of the store and a yard or so down the sidewalk where I'd parked earlier before starting my shift. Sure enough, she'd keyed it. She'd actually keyed the hell out of it, scratching the word *SLUT* in big capital letters, and it looked as if she'd dug the key as deep into the metal as she could get it.

"What the hell?" I screeched as I turned back to look at the culprit.

The contrition that had been on her face when she was focusing on her grandmother quickly shifted to a nasty, pinched looked of pure hatred as she zeroed her focus on me.

Georgia pulled in a sharp gasp as she read the ugly word carved across both doors on the driver side. "You did this to Luna's car? But . . . *why*?"

That was also something I desperately wanted to know. "Because she deserved it," the little urchin hissed. "She *is* a slut. I know because she screwed my dad."

Oh, fresh hell. I guess that answered the question about how much she'd overheard between her father and me the other day.

Cheyanne acted fast, herding us back toward the store. "I think we should take this back inside," she insisted, placing her hands on my shoulders and giving me a little nudge since I seemed to have lost the ability to speak or move on my own. Hell, I could barely hear over the sound of a trillion bees buzzing in my ears.

Dezzy rushed out from the back once everyone had gathered inside again. *Great,* I thought. *Just what I need, more people.* "What's going on?" he asked anxiously, his gaze darting between the cop in the room and everyone else. "Is someone hurt?"

Just my car, in a way I couldn't possibly afford to fix.

I was having an out of body experience, hovering over the entire group and watching from above as Georgia lifted a trembling hand to her forehead. "I can't—I don't—I'm not even sure where to start. Evan Warren, I cannot *believe* you would do something like this!"

"She started it by having sex with my dad!" the little hoodlum defended at the top of her lungs. Thank the good Lord above we didn't have any customers at the moment to overhear; it was bad enough she was saying this in front of Georgia and Dezzy. I couldn't imagine this was something I'd ever hear the end of. "He's barely been divorced, and she just jumped right into bed with him."

Georgia looked at me with big, round eyes, that, I swear to God, looked like they were shimmering with a hint of excitement. "Is this true, honey? Are you and Nate involved?" She clasped her hands in front of her chest in a gesture of hope, and I felt like such an asshole, knowing I was going to have to disappoint her.

Why, why, *why* didn't the ground open up and swallow a person whole when they desperately needed it to?

"It's not like that, Georgia. It was just—" I was about to say "a one-time thing" when I remembered that we had relatively young ears still in the room. My gaze bounced between Evan and Georgia before I lowered my voice and said, "I promise to explain everything . . . later."

Desmond came over, crossing his arms over his chest and giving the coldest, hardest, disappointed father—or in this case, grandfather—look I'd ever seen him give. "Explain yourself, missy."

The kid's chin wobbled, but I struggled to find sympathy as one tear, then a second broke free. "I didn't plan to do it. I was just walking by, and I saw her through the front window, and I know she hooked up with my dad, and I wanted so badly for him and my mom to get back together, but if he's sleeping with another woman, I know there's no way that's ever going to happen." She'd spit all that out so fast she had to pause and take a breath. "I got so mad, and I know what her car looks like, because I saw it when she came into Dad's office a few days ago. And . . ." Her shoulders fell and her head dropped forward as she ended on a whisper, "It just happened."

Once she finished with her pathetic excuse for a defense, everyone of legal drinking age looked at me.

"Well, looks like this is up to you, Luna," Sheriff Michaels drew out.

My eyes widened and darted around the room. "Looks like what's up to me?"

"The decision is yours to make. The damage to your car is gonna cost you a pretty penny. You want to press charges or not?"

Well shit.

Twelve

NATE

I'D BEEN in the middle of interviewing an eighty-four-year-old octogenarian for the position of executive assistant when I got a call that made my heart fall right out of my chest. I hadn't gotten all the details from my mother on the phone, but the mention of Evan, vandalism, and sheriff's department was more than enough to set me off. I quickly ended the interview with Ms. Dempsey, a former high school English teacher who wasn't enjoying retirement as much as she'd thought she would. I hadn't been sure, but I could have sworn Ms. Dempsey taught at the high school back when I'd attended years ago, and if I'd been right, the woman had been old as dirt even back then.

By the time I pulled up in front of my parents' store, parking beside the sheriff-department-issued cruiser, a haze of rage covered my vision so vividly, the whole world was covered in an eerie red glow.

I pushed through the door, setting off the pleasant chime of the bell that didn't fit the current situation at all. My gaze darted around the space furiously as I looked for my daughter. "Where is she?" I asked through gritted teeth, my jaw ticking manically.

"In the back office," my father answered. "We figured it best that we discuss how to handle this situation without her present."

"Agreed. So tell me what happened." My gaze passed to my mother. "You said she defaced private property? What did she do, spray paint something?"

Luna, who'd been standing off to the side, let out a derisive snort and shook her head. "Nothing so amateurish. I'll tell you, when your girl decides to do something, she goes big."

"What the hell are you doing here?" I blurted before I could stop myself.

"Nathanial Desmond Warren," my mother scolded instantly. "That is *not* how you talk to someone ever, but especially when they're the wronged party."

Ah, Christ. This isn't going to be good, I told myself, and not only because the sight of Luna Copeland caused the blood in my veins to rush so damn fast it made my skin heat. Even with the killing look she currently had pinned to her face, she was gorgeous. And not the typical kind of gorgeous either, but the kind that drew in artists, painters and sculptors, people who'd give their left foot for the chance to immortalize a face like hers.

Her skin, that creamy pale white, the kind that burned beneath the sun if she wasn't careful, turned pink with emotion. Her full rose-hued lips were pursed, and her delicate nose, slightly upturned at the very tip, was scrunched in displeasure. Even though it certainly wasn't an expression that should make a man hard, there I was, trying to fight back an erection like a goddamn teenager as I recalled our one and only night together.

I arched my brows and asked, "The wronged party?"

"She . . . keyed a defamatory word into the side of Luna's car."

Fuck. Fucking me. Fuck, fuck, fuck! "What word?"

My mother blushed, my father glanced to his shoes, color leaching from his face. When it became obvious no one else was going to chime in, Luna spoke again. "It reads *slut* in big capital letters from the front panel to the back door."

I choked on my own goddamn spit, nearly hacking up a lung. "I'm sorry, she wrote *what*?" I croaked once I was able to breathe again.

"Slut," Luna repeated. "She called me a slut; a woman she doesn't know from Adam, a complete and total stranger, all because I slept with her father." She held a finger in the air, her smile a bit manic as she added, "News that she also found okay to share with whoever was near when she got caught. And she didn't just key it. Oh no. She really gouged that sucker in deep."

I was going to kill her. That was all there was to it. My daughter was a dead girl walking.

"Luna . . . shit. I don't know what to say. I'm so sorry she did that."

"Not you who should be apologizing, son," my father grunted.

The man in the very official looking uniform spoke then, drawing my attention to him. "Glad to see you're back, Nate. Just hate the first time we're running into each other is under these circumstances."

I furrowed my brow, trying to place his face before it hit me. "Holy shit. Cade? Kincade Michaels?"

"One and the same." The corner of his mouth curled up in a small facsimile of a grin as he held his hand out. I took it, the shake hearty and friendly before he pulled me in for a quick slap on the back.

I let out a small, bewildered laugh as I took in the uniform one more time. "Damn, man. You work for the sheriff's department? I can't believe someone actually gave you a gun."

He chuckled lazily, lifting his hand to rub the back of

his neck. "Don't just work there, bud. Was actually voted in as sheriff in the last election."

"No joke?" I smiled big, going in for another back pat. "Congratulations, man. That's awesome."

"Um, excuse me," a very feminine and extremely pissed off voice cut in. "If you guys want to bro down, I'm totally fine with that, as long as you do it on your time. But we have a situation here that needs to be dealt with."

Shame crept up from my chest, heating my skin as it traveled higher and higher. I'd never felt like a bigger failure in my entire life. I'd failed as a father. No matter how hard I tried, I couldn't get through to my own daughter. I couldn't get her to talk to me, to open up, so everything she was feeling stayed locked inside, festering and festering until it exploded in a toxic and extreme way.

"Of course. Luna . . . *Christ*. I'm sorry. And please know that I'll pay to have your car repaired immediately." Reaching up, I dragged my fingers through my hair in frustration, at a loss as to what to do. "And I understand if you feel that's not good enough. The choice is yours if you want to take legal action." At those words, I could actually feel bile creeping up my throat, threatening to choke me. Did Evan have any idea how serious what she'd just done was? "I won't try to talk you out of it—"

She cut me off, something flitting across her features that sent a shiver down my spine. "I've given it some thought while you were on your way over here, and I think I've figured out a way to handle this without bringing the law into play and potentially screwing up a young kid's life."

"Oh?" I asked hesitantly. "How's that?"

"Well, first of all, you're definitely paying to fix my car, just like you said. But there's something else I want along with that. We'll call it payment for emotional distress if that helps."

"I'm almost afraid to ask," I deadpanned, prepared to have this woman rake me over the coals.

Her smile was downright smug as she sauntered up to me, stopping a few feet away. "You're going to hire me as your assistant."

Jesus, God. And the hits just kept on coming.

Except for Evan's sniffles and quiet crying, the first five minutes of the car ride home were made in silence. Usually, my daughter's tears were enough to undo me, and I wasn't too stupid to admit I was part of the problem in that sense, since I hated to see her cry and did whatever it took to put a smile back on her face, but, they didn't faze me in the slightest. I was too pissed off to feel anything else.

I had to hand it to her, Luna Copeland had finagled that whole disastrous situation like a pro. She'd not only walked away with a brand-new job—and I wasn't speaking of the paint variety that her car would be getting in the very near future—but she'd also haggled the ten paid days off I offered yearly up to two full weeks and bumped the starting pay an additional ten percent. Given how everything had taken place in front of witnesses—one of them being an enforcer of the law—she knew good and well that, unless she did something downright terrible, I was stuck with her.

She'd backed me into a corner, and if there was one thing I hated, it was being backed into a fucking corner.

I was silently seething over the recent turn of events when Evan finally worked up the courage to speak. "Daddy, I'm really sorry," she said quietly, her voice broken and watery. "I didn't mean—"

"Don't," I snapped, feeling the hold I had on my control start to slip despite her finally dropping the *Nate* bullshit and calling me daddy again. "I don't want to hear excuses. You fucked up; right thing to do is own it, so own it. Don't tell me you didn't mean to do it, because we both know that isn't true. You had four freaking letters to stop yourself, for Christ's sake. Take responsibility for your actions."

She shocked the hell out of me by sniffling and whispering, "You're right. I'm sorry."

If only that was enough, *anywhere* near enough, to make up for what she'd done. "What the hell were you thinking?" I asked, the one question that had been beating around inside my skull since I found out what she'd done. "The girl I know, the one I raised to do the right thing, would *never* go out of her way to hurt a person the way you did today. You don't even know her." She began to cry even harder, but I would not be swayed, not this time. "What in the world possessed you to call a complete stranger such a vile, despicable name?"

"I know it was wrong. I hate that I did something like that to someone Grandma and Grandpa like so much. If they like her, she can't be all bad. I just saw her, and I thought of how there's no chance of you ever getting back together with Mom if you're . . . you know . . . with other women. And I just got so mad."

I pulled into the designated parking spot I paid extra for every month and threw my car into park before turning to look at my daughter. "Jesus, Evan, please listen to me. *Hear* me. Whether or not something was actually happening between me and Ms. Copeland, or another woman, it wouldn't matter. You mother and I aren't getting back together, sweetheart. I know that was a hope you held on to while we were going through the divorce, but you have to let it go. It's never going to happen. Your mom and I, we didn't make each other happy. Now that we're no longer together, maybe we both have a shot at finding some of that happy. Wouldn't you want that for us?"

She let out a hiccup and reached up to bat at the tears streaking her cheeks with the heels of her palms, keeping her focus on her lap. "I do," she said so softly it was a wonder I heard her over the air conditioner. "And I know you're happier now." She looked at me with those big blue eyes, tears swimming, and I had to fight back the desire to tell her it was all okay, that everything would work out, that I forgave her. "I really am sorry."

My brows crept higher. "Sorry you did it, or sorry you got caught?"

I caught the small wince that swept across her face before she looked down at her lap, tugging at a loose thread on the cuff of her hoodie. "Maybe a little of both," she muttered. "What happens now? Is that lady going to press charges?" There was no mistaking the tremble of fear in my daughter' voice.

I pulled in a deep breath and laid it all out for her, everything I discussed with my parents and Luna. The agreement we came to wasn't going to make Evan happy, that was for damn sure, but it was better than legal action, hands down.

"I think it goes without saying that you're grounded."

"For how long?"

"I was leaning toward forever, but your grandparents talked me into a month."

Her eyes went so wide I was almost afraid they'd fall right out of her skull. "A *month*? That's—" she squeaked, but when I cut my eyes at her, she swallowed thickly. "That's total fair."

"Damn straight it is. That means no TV, no phone, no computer or tablet. You get to go old school and read books. And you're going to be working at the general store after school and on weekends until you've paid off the cost of the damage you did to Ms. Copeland's car."

Her mouth fell open, aghast. "So I have to work there *for free*?"

My brows fell into a straight line, my eyes narrowing in what I dubbed the Don't-Mess-With-Me dad look. As usual, that look had her clamping her mouth shut. "Damn straight you're working for free, and it's going to take you a good long while to pay off what you did. But that's not all."

She made a sound between a scoff and a choke. "What else?"

"Once a month you're going to clean Ms. Copeland's house from top to bottom. And you're damn well going to do a good job," I added quickly when it looked like she was about to argue. "None of this is up for discussion or bargaining. It's this, or she presses charges." I looked at my daughter sternly as she crossed her arms over her chest and sunk back deeper into her seat with a pout. "What's it going to be?"

She chewed on her bottom lip so hard I wondered how it wasn't bleeding before finally answering. "I guess I don't have much of a choice, huh?"

"Not one bit." I shot her a wicked smirk. "Welcome to the consequences of your actions, sweetheart. They're going to suck."

Thirteen

LUNA

I walked into the Drip to the sound of whistles and cat calls, courtesy of Monica. "Look at you! You're like the hot, curvy librarian all teenage boys wish they had working at their high school."

I grinned, my face heating from the attention my friend had just drawn as I made my way to the counter. "It's not too much?" I asked, running a hand along my front to brush at the non-existent wrinkles. The top was a bright candy apple red that might have looked plain if not for the adorable eyelet sleeves. I wore it tucked into a high-waisted black pencil skirt that hit just below my knees, and paired the whole outfit with round-toed sling-backs with pencil-thin three-inch heels.

It had taken some serious cajoling on Cheyanne's part, but I'd eventually caved and let her take me on a mini-shopping spree so I could get a suitable wardrobe for my new job. I would have gladly paid for it myself, but until my paychecks started coming in, there was no way I could have afforded it. Then there was the small matter of most of my business clothes either not fitting thanks to the stress pounds I'd put on or being on consignment shop racks waiting to be purchased second-hand so I could have some extra cash.

"Are you kidding? The red is so bold and fun. And I'd kill for your ass in that skirt."

"It's my first day at a new job, Mon. This isn't about my ass looking good. I want to make sure I look professional."

"You do. Absolutely," she assured me. "You look like a professional hot, curvy librarian straight out of a teenage boy's fantasy."

I snatched one of the wrapped straws out of the holder on the counter and aimed at her forehead, missing the mark when it caught air and veered to the left. "It's not about that!"

She cut her eyes at me, her expression screaming, *girl, who you fooling?* "Of course it's not. Because you don't care about looking good in front of the tall, built, ten-years-from-certified-silver-fox attorney." She snapped her fingers sarcastically. "Oh wait, you've already been there and done that."

My expression fell, my features going blank. "Should have known that particular bit of gossip's already started its journey down the grapevine."

Monica leaned forward, bracing her elbow on the counter, and rested her chin in her palm. "Oh, sweetie. It's been three days. That juicy little nugget's already made it to the end of that vine and is on its return trip, hitting up extra stops along the way. *Everyone's* talking about it." She lowered her voice to a conspiratorial whisper and waggled her brows. "I have to know; how was he? Those serious starched-collar types are usually the biggest freaks in the bedroom."

My face felt like it was about to catch fire, and I was certain my cheeks had to be the color of my shirt. I felt a small twinge between my thighs, my nipples stiffening into diamond points, as the memories of our night at the inn flashed through my brain. *Jesus*, what the hell was wrong with me? The man had proven himself to be a grade A, prime one asshole of the highest order, and if that wasn't bad enough, his little felon daughter wasn't much better.

"I knew it!" Monica whisper-yelled, pointing at my face. "He totally rocked your world! That's why you're all flushed right now, isn't it; because you're remembering?"

"I hate you so much," I hissed. "And I'm telling Sam you're overly interested in my sex life."

"Meh." She shrugged like it was nothing. "My man

takes care of things at home, believe me." She gave me another eyebrow waggle that made me laugh. "But we're the boring married couple now."

"I highly doubt there's anything boring about your relationship." Fact of the matter was, Sam Killborne had been labeled Whitecap's most eligible bachelor when he moved to town years ago. With his looks, his build, and the fact that he was a former professional football player, the single ladies in town had gone a little insane in their competition to catch the man's eye; not that any of them held a candle to my girl, Monica. "They'd been married nearly a decade now, and I was convinced that #relationshipgoals had been created just for them.

Her features softened, her eyes glazing over dreamily. "This is very true. Okay, so I'm just nosy. Also, I want all my friends to find their happily ever afters like I did with Sam. Cheyanne's got Trent, and the two of them are so sickeningly adorable I could puke, so now I'm shifting my focus to you."

"Well, you can take that focus, turn it around, and send it right the hell back where it came from. You know my rule."

Monica held up her hands grudgingly. "Yeah, yeah. You don't do relationships."

I nodded briskly. "That's right. No relationships." I let out a grumble as she made my usual coffee. "Believe me, if

I'd had any clue who he really was, I wouldn't have touched him with a ten-foot pole."

But then I wouldn't have gotten to experience that once-in-a-lifetime unicorn sex, I reminded myself silently.

Monica blew out a raspberry and set my drink in front of me. "Sure, keep telling yourself that. But I swear to God, one of these days you're going to meet someone who knocks you flat on your ass, and I'm going to be right there to say 'I told you so' when it happens."

I took my first fortifying sip of that blessed caffeine before giving her a big, cheesy grin. "I'd expect nothing less. I'm off! Have to hustle so I'm not late for my first day."

"Good luck!" she called, waving after me as I sauntered out of the coffee shop on my new heels. "You're going to slay it, babe!"

I cruised along Water Street with the sun shining brightly through the windshield of the zippy new rental car I'd be driving around until mine got out of the shop. I found a place to park about half a block from the cheery yellow house-turned-law-firm and climbed out, hooking my purse on my shoulder before beeping the locks and heading toward my new workplace.

The grass was still lush and emerald green. The flowers in the beds were still vibrant as I made my way up the front walk. I'd half expected the door to be locked, and let out what I hoped was a subtle sigh of relief when it pulled right open and I was greeted by the welcoming coolness of air conditioning inside.

My heels clicked on the parquet floor as I stepped across the threshold and started in the direction of the empty desk I'd seen last time I was here. "Hello?" I called out, proud that the nerves I felt fluttering in my belly didn't come through in my voice.

Nate stepped out of his office, a finely built man of six-plus-feet in a bespoke suit that made my belly quiver the moment I laid eyes on him. His button-down shirt was a light blue this morning, tucked into a pair of navy slacks. His brown leather belt matched his dress shoes to perfection, both of which cost a pretty penny. He'd stripped off the jacket at some point after arriving, and I noticed that, just like the day I'd come in for my disastrous interview, he was without a tie, the top button of his collar undone.

It really was cruel for a man to look that damn good. I'd heard mention from Georgia that he was forty—eleven years older than I was, not that he looked it, the stupid jerk. I didn't have the first clue what he looked like when he was younger, but looking at him now, it was obvious the asshole had only gotten better with age.

"Nice of you to finally make it," he groused.

I made a show of slowly lifting and twisting my arm so I could look down at my watch then back to him, raising an obstinate brow. "Start time is eight o'clock. It's seven fifty-seven."

He grumbled something under his breath I couldn't quite make out, but it didn't take a rocket scientist to realize he wasn't complimenting me. "Fine, let's get started then."

"Sounds good," I said with enthusiasm. "I take it this is mine?" I pointed at the long white desk stationed between his office and the restroom. He grunted in the affirmative, so I quickly rounded it and dropped my purse on top, rummaging around inside for my tablet. I pressed the button to bring the screen to life, pulling up the notes app, and shifted my focus back to Nate. "Ready."

"First thing each morning, I'll expect a cup of coffee. Black, two sugars." I paused in my tapping, lifting my head and blinking slowly. Was he kidding? I was an executive assistant in charge of managing the entirety of his office so he could focus on his case work, and he was talking to me about coffee? "I usually work through lunch, so around eleven thirty, I'll expect you to run out and grab me something to eat."

I narrowed my eyes. I knew what this guy was doing. He was being a dick in the hopes he could push me to quit, but he didn't know the first thing about me. I was going to stick to this job like fucking glue.

I quickly tapped out a short note on my tablet before

shifting my attention back to him. "Coffee and lunch. Got it. What's next?"

The skin between his brows crinkled as he frowned, clearly having expected a very different reaction from me. "I'll need you to call and have the phone lines set up. The internet needs connected. Research different payroll software and give me a list of the top three and the reasons why you chose them so I can look it over and decide. Find a printer in the area and order business cards. I'll write out what I want on them. Then draft an ad to put in the local paper and on Whitecap's social media, announcing we're open for business. Then there are the office supplies . . . get them."

My fingers that had been flying over my tablet at lightning speed as he rattled off one task after another stopped abruptly at that vague instruction. "Which ones?"

"All of them." A small, wicked grin tugged his lips up. "If you're as good as you claim to be, there's no reason you can't get that all done before lunch. After that, you can start on the filing."

Stick like fucking glue, I chanted in my head. I could do this. I *would* do this. I could somehow cram an entire day's work into a few measly hours. I was going to make this asshole regret ever trying to run me off.

"Got it. What kind of filing system is in place now?"

For some reason, that question made him smirk in a

way that sent a shiver down my spine, and *not* in a good way. "You'll see for yourself. You'll find everything you need in the conference room upstairs." He spun on the heel of his shoe and started back for his office, calling over his shoulder. "Now get to work. And get me that coffee."

Oh, I'd get him his coffee, all right. But there was definitely going to be a little something extra in it.

Fourteen

NATE

MY ANNOYANCE BLOOMED BRIGHTER and larger with every minute that ticked by until I could feel the vein in my forehead throb. All because my plan hadn't worked. If anything, it had backfired, biting me right in the ass.

It was bad enough I was still hot over being forced to hire her in the first damn place, all because she'd successfully managed to tie my hands behind my back, but then she'd walked in here in that outfit, and every bit of saliva in my mouth dried up. I thought I'd remembered our night together in such vivid detail I could have sketched it to perfection if I had the faintest clue how to draw, then she'd turned around and I saw how that skirt hugged that firm, round ass to perfection, and I realized what I'd remembered had been seriously watered down.

Her siren-red hair hung past her shoulders in thick,

silky waves, and the small bit of makeup she was wearing highlighted the delicate, feminine features of her face, enhancing the natural beauty that lay beneath.

And damn if the perfume she was wearing didn't smell so fucking good. My ex had always talked about how a woman should have a signature scent. Unfortunately, the one she'd chosen reminded me of a funeral parlor stuffed to the gills with old potpourri. That cloying, powdery smell was so damn strong I swore I tasted it whenever she walked by, like chalk and my grandma's closet. But Luna's scent was completely different. For one, it was much subtler than the choking mothballs my ex wore constantly, and I had to say, it was nice not to be slapped in the face with perfume every time I turned the corner.

At one point during our night together, I'd buried my face in her neck and pulled in long, deep breaths, trying to identify the fragrance, but I couldn't figure it out. And I still couldn't. It was sweet but with an undertone of musk. There was a warmth to it that reminded me of the scotch I'd drunk the first night we met. It smelled like sin and heaven, and the longer she walked around the small building, the more likely it would seep into the walls until there was nowhere I could go that didn't smell like her. It was even in my office from when she'd brought me my coffee earlier, for Christ's sake.

I had to get rid of her. With everything happening

with Evan, the last thing I could afford to do was complicate my life even more by working with someone I'd slept with. Spending day in and day out with a woman whose body I'd spent hours getting to know. Being stuck in the same damn room with the very person I couldn't stop thinking about. And Christ, now I was hard. Just fucking perfect.

I'd walked back into my office earlier after giving Luna her list of tasks, feeling smug as hell, so damn sure my unreasonable demands and surly attitude would be more than enough to run her off. I'd half expected to hear the click of those sexy-as-fuck heels on the wood floors as she stormed out the door, never to return. There was no way anyone could possibly accomplish everything I'd given her in the time I'd allotted. It wasn't only impossible; it was downright insane. Not to mention, a dick move.

But somehow, damn it, she'd pulled it off. The internet and phone hookup alone should have set her back. I knew because I'd already called and been told the techs wouldn't be able to get out to my office for another week.

I'd chuckled to myself when I heard her on the phone earlier—her cell since the office lines weren't set up— attempting to sweettalk the internet provider into getting out here that morning to get things up and running.

Good luck, I'd thought to myself at the time. So, you

could imagine my surprise when, barely an hour later, there was some dude in a navy polo and trousers walking past my office.

"Arnie, you're an absolute lifesaver," Luna cooed as the guy got to work on the phones *and* the internet. "I really owe you one for coming out on such short notice."

"Nothing to thank me for, Lu. It's what we do around here," the guy returned. Goddamn small towns. I'd forgotten about the whole help-a-neighbor-in-need thing, something seriously lacking in the big cities.

"Still. I really appreciate it. I owe you, big time. First round's on me next time we hit the Dropped Anchor."

"You got it."

I'd shot up from my desk after that and slammed my door shut so I could work in peace.

Not long after the Wi-Fi was hooked up, I got an email alert on my phone.

Below are a few different versions of the ad text you wanted for the paper and social media. Please let me know if any of these work for you and I'll get everything sent to the proper people.

Luna Copeland,

Executive Assistant Extraordinaire

I almost didn't catch the laugh that bubbled up at her signature. The last thing I needed was for her to think I enjoyed anything about her, but I had to admit, she was pretty damn clever. And all three samples of the ad text were perfect. *Damn it.*

Apparently, that small town hospitality extended to the office supplies too, because shortly before 11:00, a delivery guy showed up with a whole van full of supplies from a local shop downtown.

When noon rolled around and there was no word on the business cards—which could take days or weeks to come in—or the payroll software, a Grinchy smirk curled at my lips. I might not have been able to fire her for something so minor, but I could sure as hell make her life here a living hell until she decided to quit all on her own, and this was the perfect ammunition I needed.

To be an asshole, I summoned her to my office by bellowing her name like I'd been raised with no manners whatsoever. A moment later she stepped into my office, the picture of calm, cool, and professional.

"I thought I told you I wanted your research on payroll software before lunch." I gestured exaggeratedly at the computer on my desk—that could now connect to the internet, but whatever—and noted the time. "It's noon. Officially lunch time by most American standards."

"I have the research on my computer and would be glad to email it to you for your records, but I already went ahead and purchased the software." I opened my mouth, ready to let her have it, when she continued. "I'd already looked through all the software out there back when I started my own company, so I had a pretty good idea of the one that would fit your needs. It's cheaper than the other programs you see ads for, and it doesn't have all the bells and whistles, but that's because you don't need the bells and whistles yet. Until the firm gets up and running to the point you need to bring on more personnel, you'd just be throwing money down the drain with those other programs, and since I signed us up to pay the yearly subscription fees, we got an additional discount."

Son of a bitch. Okay, so she was efficient. So what? It didn't change the fact that I'd seen her naked and just the memory of it made my dick hard. We could *not* work together, goddamn it!

"And I know you didn't mention it, but the program I got helps with keeping everything in line for tax season, and when the time comes, we can also send client invoices and receive payment through it as well. One-stop-shop to keep things streamlined and simplified. Oh, and the print shop should have your business cards ready by the end of the day."

My mouth dropped open. "How—?"

"They're local. I helped create their website at a discounted rate when they were first starting out, so I was able to call in a favor. It's owned by the sweetest couple. Anyway, I put in an order for four hundred. If that's not enough, you just let me know and I'll put in another call. That might take a couple days though. I don't think my favor will extend that far."

"I—no—I mean, four hundred is fine. For now." I was just about to play my last card—my late lunch—when a voice I didn't recognize called out from the front of the building.

"Hello?"

Luna's face brightened considerably with a smile that made my chest clench as she called back, "Oh, Tony, perfect timing! We're back here."

"Who the hell's Tony?" I murmured.

"Tony Rizzoli from Rizzoli's Pies. Best pizza in Oregon. Best subs too." Just then, a welcomed blast from the past stepped into the doorway.

"Well, if it isn't little Natey Boy."

"Tony Rizzoli!"

Luna's gaze bounced between Tony and me. "You two know each other?"

"We don't just know each other. I gave Nate here his first job back when he was in high school. It's been too long, son."

I stood from my chair on a hearty laugh and rounded my desk, meeting Tony halfway across the room for a sturdy man-hug, complete with back slap. "That it has, old man," I said jovially as I stepped back so I could get a good look at him. Now in his sixties, he still had the same deep olive complexion, the same bright, smiling brown eyes, but time had thinned his once dark hair and painted it liberally with silver. The laugh lines around his eyes had deepened a bit, and while he still maintained that stocky build, he'd softened a touch around the middle.

"Who you calling old? I could still take you on any day of the week." He balled his fists and pretended to give my gut a couple jabs for good measure.

"I don't doubt that. Man, it's good to see you." I sniffed the air, the familiar scent coming back to me in an instant. "And your meatball parm still smells like heaven," I said as I glanced down at the white plastic sack he was holding, the handles straining under the weight of the two subs inside. Tony didn't skimp on his sandwiches. He loaded his sub with so many meatballs it was heavy as a damn brick.

"Damn straight it does. Tastes like it too." He turned to Luna, and I could have sworn the man got stars in his eyes for a moment. "Little moonbeam here called in a lunch order for pick-up, but I saw who it was for and figured I'd make the delivery myself, stop in to officially welcome you home."

"I'm sorry I haven't been by. Things have been a bit crazy since I got back."

He lifted his bushy caterpillar eyebrows. "I might have heard something about that."

Ah, the small-town grapevine hard at work. This was going to be a fucking nightmare.

"Also heard you're taking care of it, which shows you're a good man."

Luna let out a snort that she tried to cover up with a cough. "Sorry. Allergies. I think the pollen count's high today."

I shot her a glare when Tony wasn't looking, and in return, the harpy stuck out her tongue. Pollen my ass.

"Well, I'm sure you two are busy, so this old man'll get out of your hair."

"It was good seeing you again, Tony. I promise I won't be a stranger," I said, giving him a clap on the shoulder.

"You make sure you don't." He reached out and placed his hand on Luna's arm. "And be good to this one, yeah? She one of the best out there. You really lucked out, getting her on your team."

Luna beamed proudly at my old boss. "Thank you,

Tony. For the compliment and for delivering our lunch." She took the bag from his hand and leaned in to place a kiss on his cheek, and if I wasn't mistaken, the man actually blushed.

She waited until he was gone before turning on her heel, looking far too happy with herself. "Well, boss. If you don't need anything else, I'm going to enjoy my lunch break. Then I have some filing to do."

She sauntered out of my office, whistling a happy little tune as her tantalizing ass swayed from side to side with each step.

This was my worst nightmare.

Fifteen

LUNA

By day three at my new job, I was starting to wonder if I was the type of person who could get away with murdering my new boss and disposing of his body. I'd watched enough true crime that I thought I had a pretty good handle on what *not* to do, but I wasn't sure yet if I had the disposition for homicide. However, the more he pushed, the more likely I was to get there, that was for damn sure. The man had gone out of his way to make my life a complete misery between the hours of eight and five.

Keeping my composure while secretly wanting to jab a pencil into the man's eye was getting harder and harder. He fought me every step of the way on everything I did, from converting his joke of a filing system to digital in an effort to free up space and boost him into the twenty-first century, to the type of Post-It notes I'd stocked—he hated the pop-up style ones and thought the bright colors were childish and ridiculous.

I worked tirelessly to prove I could do a good job, reminding myself over and over that my first paycheck was still a week and a half away, but sometimes even that didn't feel like enough to keep me from losing my cool.

If he wasn't riding me about the million and one things he thought I was doing wrong, he was complaining. Complaining about the kind of work he was getting now that we were officially open for business and taking on clients, complaining about the lack of delivery options in such a small town, complaining about the fact that most everyone who walked into the office already knew the gist of our first meeting. It was one thing after another until I was convinced the man just didn't know how to be happy.

Ignoring his tantrums seemed to be the only thing that worked, so on day four, I rerouted all the calls that would come in at my desk to the phone in the conference room up in the loft area on the second floor, and buried myself in work, digging through the boxes of files—Nate's current and inefficient system—and scanning each and every page into the digital folder I'd created.

I'd been so lost in my work that I'd lost track of time as the hours rushed by. With the very last document scanned and digitally put in place, I closed the lid of the very last file box with smile, a firm sense of accomplishment making my chest feel light and loose. Pumped on adrenaline from finishing the most boring, menial task in the world, I hefted the closest box up and started down the stairs with it. *One down, only fifteen more to go*, I thought as I hit the landing.

"Jesus Christ, what are you doing? You're going to fall and break your neck."

"Ha! I wouldn't give you the satisfaction," I replied right before Nate rushed over and yanked the box out of my hands. I let out a breath, shaking out my straining arms. I wasn't really hip on cardio, but if doing this meant I didn't have to hit the gym or go for a run, I'd take it. "Thanks. If you'll just put that by the door, I'll go up and grab another." I turned on my heel—open-toed in a soft bone color this time—and reached for the stair railing.

"Nuh-uh, no way." He braced the cardboard box on his hip and under one arm, like it weighed next to nothing, and grabbed my wrist before I could take a step, preventing me from moving. I flinched at the electric shock his touch sent across my skin, and my gaze shot down to where his long fingers wrapped around my wrist, making it look positively dainty. I was suddenly very aware of his hands in a way I'd never been aware of that appendage on another person before. He had nice, well-shaped nail beds and short, blunt, clean fingernails. There was still the faintest pale band on his finger from the wedding ring he'd worn for years before his divorce, and when the hell did I start finding a man's hands attractive?

I managed to shake my head clear of the unexpected daze as he continued in that brusque tone he always used with me. "You aren't carrying boxes down these stairs." He jerked his chin at my feet. "Especially in those shoes. That's a worker's comp claim just waiting to happen."

I forced an eyeroll, hoping the strange reaction I'd just had to his touch didn't show on my face as I pulled my arm from his grip. "Oh, give me a break. I'll be fine, thank you very much. I used to live in heels. I assure you, I can navigate a flight of stairs no problem."

He gave his head an abrupt shake. "Not with a box. No way. You need something moved, I'll do it." He registered the box in his arms then. "Speaking of, what the hell are you doing with my files anyway?"

"I found a company that does offsite archiving and shredding. I've scheduled them to pick the boxes up and store them at their facility until you go through the digital files I created and decide what you need to keep hard copies of and what you don't. If something comes up and you need an old file in hand, all I have to do is fill something out on their website and they'll deliver what we need back to us. Simple, efficient, and a huge space-saver given we don't have much square footage here."

"That's . . . actually pretty smart." I nearly laughed at

the sour, sickly look on his face, as if admitting I'd done something right made him physically ill.

"I know. I'm full of brilliant ideas. Do you need to sit down after saying that? You look like you're about to throw up."

He let out a *humph*, muttering under his breath as he turned and carried the box toward the front of the office. "Don't you touch those boxes," he called back at me. "I'll handle them myself."

If he wanted to handle the manual labor, he wasn't going to get any complaints from me.

I left work right at five and drove straight to Warren's General Store. It had been a difficult day in a week of difficult days, thanks to my new boss, and I planned to treat myself to a night of relaxation with a bottle of wine, a steamy bubble bath, and my latest romance audio book.

"Hey, honey," Georgia greeted over the soft tinkling of the bell over the door. "How're you doing?"

I changed direction, heading toward the register where she sat instead of the wine aisle. "Fine. Exhausted. In desperate need of wine after the day I've had."

Her face pulled into a look of concern. "Everything

okay? That boy of mine isn't making things hard for you, is he?"

"No," I assured her with a smile, even though he absolutely was. But she didn't need to know that. "Trust me, I can handle him." At least that was true. I'd learned over the past few days to just suck it up at work, then go home and scream into a pillow until spots danced in front of my vision from lack of oxygen. It was cathartic. But tonight, wine.

"Oh, honey, I know you can. If there's a woman on this continent who can handle that man, it's you. I love him, and I'm glad he's home, more than you could possibly know, but I'm not blind to the fact my son can be a pain in the rear end when he wants to be."

I lifted my brows and laughed. "Ah, so you *do* know him. And that particular want seems to be constant."

She reached across the counter and patted the back of my hand. "I have all the faith in the world you'll put him in his place." She tightened her grip as she leaned forward and lowered her voice, her eyes doing that glinting thing again. "And then, just maybe the two of you will find that spark that drew you together the first night you met."

I groaned. "Georgia, come on. Don't start with that. You know my rule. No—"

"Relationships," she finished for me, holding up her hands before clasping them together at her chest. "I know,

I know. But you'd be so cute together," she cooed. "And you'd be so good for him. I just know it."

"That's not going to happen," I insisted, then grabbed hold of the first thing I could think of to shift the topic. "How are things working out with your granddaughter as free labor?"

"Oh, it's fine," Georgia said breezily. "You may not believe it, given what she did to you, but she's not a bad kid, not at her core. Spoiled by one parent, that would be my son," she said flatly, "and all but abandoned by the other. When you look at the big picture, it's not all that surprising she's pulling the stunts she's pulling."

My curiosity was piqued and I couldn't bring myself to ignore it. I wanted to know too badly, so I rested my forearms on the counter and asked, "What's the story there? When she showed up at his office the day of my interview, she said she wasn't Nate's real daughter."

Georgia let out an aggrieved huff. "That seems to be her thing lately, that and calling him Nate instead of Dad."

Okay, even *more* curious now. "Why would she say something like that?"

Georgia didn't hesitate to explain. "Evan was already two when Nate met her momma. The relationship was okay, probably would have fizzled had it not been for the girl. He fell for Evan long before falling for her mom. That's why he stayed in it. That's why he married her. And that's why he didn't divorce her a year into the marriage like he should have. Adopted her the moment he was legally bound to her mother, already had the papers drawn up and everything before the wedding was completely planned."

My heart did a little flip, and I didn't realize I'd been holding my breath until the burn in my lungs grew too painful to ignore. I didn't want to see the guy in a different light. I was comfortable with the one currently shining on him. By keeping him tucked into the slot designated for asshole bosses, I could sometimes forget that he was the guy I'd had headboard-rattling, bedframe-breaking sex with. But I felt myself softening toward him after hearing Georgia's story, and that was *not* good.

Fortunately, I was saved from having to overthink the shit out of everything when the girl in question came around the corner that led to the back. "Grandma, I finished the stockroom. What else do—" She jerked to a stop the moment she lifted her eyes and spotted me, her skin flushing a deep pink from her neck to her cheeks. "Uh —I—You—"

I couldn't help but smile at her nervous fumbling. "Hey there, Shawshank. How's it going? Commit any felonies lately?"

Her eyes went so wide I could actually see the blue of them beneath all that inky eyeliner. Studying her just then, really studying her for the first time, I could tell, beneath the makeup and the bad attitude, Evan Warren was a cute girl; cute enough that her dad was going to have some sleepless nights when he finally started letting her date. And in a few short years, she'd be a beautiful woman. She just needed someone to guide her hand when it came to cosmetics. At the moment, however, she looked like an adorable little bunny in the middle of the road, about to be flattened by an oncoming truck. "Um, I don't —that is—"

"Oh, you knock it off." Georgia laughed and batted my arm. "You're going to give the poor girl a coronary at fourteen."

I smiled at the skittish kid and shook my head. "I'm just messing with you. You said you got that stockroom in order?"

She shifted from foot to foot, tugging nervously at the hem of the maroon Warren's General Store smock she wore over her clothes. "Um, yeah—yes. Yes ma'am."

I let out whistle. "Impressive. I've seen that room, and I know it was a disaster. You got it done fast."

The flush remained in her cheeks as she ducked her head and bit her lip to fight back her grin. "Yeah, it was pretty bad," she mumbled, reaching up to tuck her hair behind her ear.

Figuring it was time to cut the kid some slack, I turned

back to Georgia and announced, "Well, my bathtub is calling. I should grab that wine and head on home."

"Okay, sweetie. I'll ring you up just as soon as I give Evan here her next task."

From the corner of my eye, I saw the girl's shoulders droop in relief now that she knew I wasn't sticking around, and that time, I was the one ducking my head and biting my lip to fight back a smile.

Evan

I didn't realize I'd been staring at the door Ms. Copeland had exited, lost in my own head, until my grandmother tapped my shoulder and jolted me back into realty. "You okay, sweetie? I said your name three times."

My cheeks warmed at being caught. "Sorry. Guess I was lost in a daze."

She reached up and pressed her palm to my cheek. Grandma had always been so nice. From the first moment I met her and Grandpa, they'd treated me like I was their own flesh and blood, so the fact that I'd disappointed them by doing what I'd done to Ms. Copeland's car made me sick for days. Every time I thought about the looks on their faces when the sheriff had pulled me into their store, my eyes burned and welled up. It was bad enough, disappointing my dad, but them too? I'd felt like even worse crap than I had when Dad came to pick me up after we'd crashed Kelsey's mom's car. He'd rushed in, his face all white and panicked, worried I'd been hurt. I felt terrible after that, but this had been even worse.

"You know her pretty well, right?" I asked, tipping my head toward the exit. "Ms. Copeland, I mean. You're friends?"

Grandma laughed that bubbly, cheerful laugh that always made me smile. "I might be a little too old to call myself her *friend*, but yes, I know her very well. We're very close."

I chewed on my bottom lip, as I looked back outside. "So . . . she's cool then? I mean, if you and Grandpa like her so much, she must be okay."

She seemed okay just a few minutes ago. She'd smiled when she saw me come around the corner, and it wasn't a nasty smile. It had seemed genuine. I wasn't sure who Shawshank was, but I got the impression she'd been joking with me. Then she'd told me I did a good job for finishing the stockroom as fast as I did. After what I'd done, the fact she could be nice like that, she *had* to be cool. Which only made me feel worse for keying her car.

"Oh, Luna's wonderful. Kind-hearted, funny, sweet."

She gave me a serious look. "That's how I know she'll most definitely forgive you if you apologize to her."

That burn came back to my eyes, and I dropped my head to hide behind my hair.

"Oh, sweetie." Grandma took my face in her hands, forcing me to look up at her. "I know your life's been hard recently. The divorce, then your momma shipping you off." She shook her head and clucked her tongue, and I got the feeling that maybe my mom wasn't her favorite person. What I didn't say out loud was that the feeling was mutual. As much as she hurt me, as much as the last things she'd said to me made me cry, I was scared to tell Dad or my grandparents any of it. She was still my mom, and the thought of them hating her made me sick to my stomach.

"You've had to deal with a lot. But I promise you, it gets better. Take it from someone who's lived it and knows, the bumps always smooth out eventually. You just have to grit your teeth and push on."

I let out a sigh and got back to work—or punishment, more like it—thinking that I sure hoped she was right and things would start to smooth out soon.

Sixteen

LUNA

Crossing the threshold into Nate's office, I tried to take small, imperceptible breaths through my mouth, hoping that would prevent me from picking up the intoxicating scent of cloves and leather with the subtle hint of tobacco. It was a smell that was distinctly Nate and left my brain muddled every damn time I smelled it. If I were honest, just one of those three scents set off a Pavlovian response in which my nipples tightened and my mouth grew dry as lust swamped me. It had gotten so damn bad I'd had to throw the jar of cloves I'd kept in my spice rack in the garbage because I kept opening it to get a sniff.

Pathetic.

Every time I smelled it, I was transported back to the night we first met, to that shitty bar where everything was sticky and covered in a layer of grime. It was a crying shame the man turned out to be such a pompous, hard-hearted dickhead, because he still managed to rev my engine somehow. It really wasn't fair that a man who looked like that had a personality pricklier than a porcupine mating with a cactus.

I was halfway to his desk when his head came up, those eyes the color of smoke or a heavy mist, hitting me like a punch to the gut even with the space between us. They narrowed as they watched me grow closer, the ever-present furrow between his brows notching even deeper. "Why are you breathing like that?" he asked in a tone only a step or two up from accusatory.

"Like what?"

"Like you're about to hyperventilate."

Well, shit, I thought. So much for imperceptible.

"What's wrong with you? Are you sick?" From the way he shot his chair back and curled his top lip up, you'd have thought I was about to cough tuberculosis all over his desk just for the fun of it.

"No, I'm not sick," I said flatly, breathing normally now that my initial plan had failed. I'd just have to live with being able to smell him. The delicious bastard. "But your reaction would be heartwarming if I were." I tossed the thin stack of sticky notes—still brightly colored because I was standing my ground on that one—onto his desk. "Here are the messages that came in overnight. And your calendar's been updated to show your meetings for the rest of the month."

"Great," he said in a tone that indicated it was anything but as he snatched up the messages and began riffling through them. "Let's see what we've got. Will update. Will update. Will update to, and I quote, 'Make sure my lousy waste-of-oxygen son doesn't get a single red cent.' Will update. Divorce. Another will update. Divorce. And oh look." He flipped the last one around for me to see. "Someone wants to sue their HOA because they got a notice that the sculpture in their front yard is against regulation for being too vulgar. That's a new one." When he was done, he tossed the sticky notes down on the desk with a disgusted sneer.

"Jeez, what the hell crawled up your butt?"

He turned that pinch-faced look back to me. "What crawled up my butt, as you so elegantly put it, is that this wasn't exactly what I had in mind when I opened a practice in Whitecap. It's a waste of a perfectly good law degree."

It was my turn to curl my lip up in disgust. "Wow."

"What?"

I shook my head in disbelief. "Nothing, boss. I'll let you get back to it." I turned on the heel of my flirty nude stiletto and started for the door when he called my name, bringing me to a stop.

"It's obvious you have something to say, so just say it."

The odds of keeping my job after this were slim to none, but it had been three weeks of this shit. Three weeks of his childish bellyaching over his current lot in life that, at least from where I was standing, didn't seem so damn bad, and I couldn't take it for another freaking second.

Whipping back around, I cocked my hip, throwing one leg out, and planted my hands on my hips. "Okay. You asked for it." At that, the infuriating man leaned deeper into his chair, rocking it backward and resting his elbows on the arms, fingers steepled in front of his chest like he was settling in. "I am sick and tired of listening to you bitch and whine like a toddler about everything under the damn sun," I snapped. The dam inside me had broken, and every grievance, every slight I'd felt coming from him over the past two weeks came rushing out of me like a tidal wave.

"You think *you* have it bad?" I jabbed a finger in his direction with a caustic laugh. "I tried living the American dream, I tried having it all, being my own boss, a career I actually enjoyed, and I failed so spectacularly, I had to resort to working at the dive-iest of dive bars for extra cash so my water wouldn't get shut off for a *second* time. As if that wasn't humiliating enough, I'm now stuck working for a cold, callous prick I can't stand so I don't lose my house.

"And, oh! Just because that's not enough crap dumped on my life, he also happens to be a random bar hookup I was never supposed to see again. But I suck it up. I swallow all that down and wake up each morning, determined to do it all over again, because I'm not a quitter. I'm an adult with adult responsibilities. No one promised us life was going to be easy or being a grownup was going to be a barrel of fun. It's hard work. But you have to do it, so there's no use whining about it," I finished on a raised voice.

"And you think that's what I'm doing? Whining because my life's not fun?"

"Isn't it?" I challenged. "From the way people react when they see you, what they say, it's obvious when you blew out of here, you didn't bother staying in touch with the people who'd been in your life from birth. You left Whitecap in your rearview and everyone who cared about you with it. To me, that says you think you're better than this place." I crossed my arms over my chest and narrowed my eyes in challenge. "Tell me I'm wrong."

He opened his mouth to object but couldn't, because he knew I had him. So I kept on chugging right along.

"Honestly, your self-important attitude blows my mind, because Georgia and Dezzy are two of the most down-to-earth, kind-hearted, hardworking people I've ever had the privilege of knowing. How they'd create someone as entitled and selfish as you is beyond me." I clicked my tongue and shook my head, the action radiating disappointment. "But it sure makes sense to me now why your girl is the way she is. She's come by her attitude honestly. Like father, like daughter."

"You can't—"

"You told me to," I threw back in his face. "That means you get to sit there and take it." My hand shot out like a rattlesnake about to strike. I lifted the first sticky note and turned it to him. "Will update for Mrs. Sills," I read. "Might seem tedious to you, but seeing as she was just diagnosed with stage four breast cancer a couple weeks ago, I imagine it probably seems pretty serious to her."

Nate's entire frame deflated, and I knew my point had been made, but I wasn't nearly done. "And this first divorce here," I said, holding up yet another note. "This is Angela Hasky. Maybe drafting up those divorce papers is boring, but since this means she's finally summoned up the courage to leave the man who's been putting his hands on her for the past five years, I'm sure she's downright terrified but strong enough to finally, *finally* see it through."

I threw the rest of them down, scattering the brightly colored paper squares along the slick, polished wood surface of his desk. "You may think your law degree is going to waste on such menial tasks, but these are *real* people scraping together money to pay you for a job that's important to them. So you're not at some fancy, big-city firm, so the hell what? Get over it. If you'd pull that stick out of your ass long enough to look around, you'd see how great this town really is. This right here," I jabbed my finger at the messages, "is good, honest work for good, honest people. You think you're better than them? That you're above this kind of thing? Then do everyone here a favor and leave, because if that's your attitude, we don't want you here."

By the time I finished, I was breathing so heavily my chest heaved, straining the tiny buttons down the center of my soft, silky, pale pink blouse. The air in the room crackled with energy, adding a dangerous charge to the silence between us. Just when I thought I might blow my top if he didn't say *something*, he spoke.

"You finished?" Just two words. That was it.

I wasn't quite ready to lower my weapons just yet, not when I wasn't sure what was coming next. "Depends."

His fingers were still steepled, his expression still arrogant and bored, only I knew better than to believe it. Those blueish-gray eyes of his had gone from mist to storm clouds vibrating with thunder and lightning. "On?"

"On whether or not I've just lost my job."

I could have sworn I saw the quickest, smallest little flicker of amusement cross his features, but that couldn't have been right. Satan didn't have a sense of humor. "And if I said you had?"

"Then I think I'd have a bit more fuel left in the tank," I answered, my words a warning: Fire me, and I'll gladly stand here and tear into you until my tongue's lashed the meat right off your bones.

"Then I guess it's a good thing you aren't fired."

Well, that was a surprise. "Guess so."

"Then get back to work." He sat up straight, scooting his chair closer to his desk, and shifted his attention back to the computer. And just like that, I was dismissed.

I turned and started for the door again only to have him stop me by calling my name . . . again. I didn't bother turning all the way around that time, instead, opting to hold on to the power by glaring at him over my shoulder.

"You still haven't gotten me my coffee this morning. And for lunch, I'd like a burger from Joe's. Medium, add bacon, no pickles."

I blinked slowly.

"You got that?"

God, I really wish I had the power to set things on fire with my mind. "Got it," I gritted. "Anything else?"

"That's it. For now." He lowered his head to the document sitting on top of his desk as his way of dismissing me, but I could have sworn I saw a flash of a smile.

Seventeen

NATE

"Dad, do I really have to do this?" Evan whined from the passenger seat for the third time since we left the apartment and started toward the beach. "It's a Saturday."

"You do," I repeated for the third time. "And I know it's a Saturday, just like I know it wouldn't matter what day of the week it is because you're still grounded."

"For three more days," she whined. "You could have been cool and let me off early."

"Ah, but I'm not the cool, fun dad. I'm the lame dad." I shot her a wink that made her snort.

"Believe me, I know. You're totally old and nerdy." A teasing smile pulled at her lips, and just the sight of it made my chest feel light. She was still grouchy most of the time, there was no denying that, and I still couldn't do most things right, but it was like a veil had lifted over the past week or so, and I was starting to see flashes of my girl again. "It's embarrassing, really. When I'm an adult, I'm going to put you in one of those old folks' homes so I don't have to deal with you anymore."

"I feel the love," I deadpanned as I made the left turn the GPS indicated.

"Holy crap," Evan breathed, giving voice to exactly what I was thinking as we pulled up to Luna's house. My daughter leaned forward to get a better look through the windshield as I parked behind Luna's car and hit the button to kill the engine. "This place is sick. The water is like, *right there.*" She pointed out the passenger window to the stretch of sandy beach the houses backed up to. "It's big too." Her shoulders sank with that realization, the excitement of the beach being only yards away drying up. "This is going to take forever to clean."

"And remember, no cutting corners" I reminded. "You do it right the first time, or you start over again."

"Yeah, yeah," she mumbled. "I got it." She grabbed the handle and climbed out of the car just as the front door opened and Luna stepped onto the porch.

A fist slammed into my chest at the sight of her. The bright, cheerful sunshine hit her hair, making it look like waves of fire. Dressed for a casual, relaxing Saturday at home, she wore a pair of cutoff-jean shorts that showed off those long legs with miles of that creamy magnolia-white skin. She had on a faded concert tee with Guns and Roses' logo on the front, knotted just above the waistband of her shorts. Lastly, her feet were tucked into a pair of those ridiculously ugly bright pink Crocs.

There was something about seeing Luna like this, comfortable in her own skin and on her turf, the picture of relaxation, that drew me to her like a moth to a flame. I'd planned to drop Evan off and be on my way, but instead, I followed my daughter's lead and got out, trailing behind her as she started up the crushed shell driveway.

This was the Luna I'd met that first night at the bar. The real Luna, in her element, and it was just as intoxicating now as it had been in that dive bar.

She surprised me even further by smiling at Evan with ease. "Hey, you guys made it. Hope you found it okay."

"Yeah, it was easy," Evan answered, her voice slightly timid but a lot curious. "So, you live on the beach. That's pretty cool."

Luna's smile grew even bigger. "Well, not *right* on it. There's a greenbelt between the property lines and the beach in this neighborhood, but it's pretty small."

From what we could see around the front of the house, that greenbelt couldn't have been more than thirty yards wide.

"Now, my friend Cheyanne, her place is literally on the

beach. You walk out her back gate and you're standing on sand."

Evan blinked. "Yeah, but your place is really nice, too. We just live in a small apartment. You can see the water from our balcony, but only because we're on the third floor. Otherwise, the view would be of a parking lot."

"I said it's temporary, didn't I?" I chimed in, bumping Evan's shoulder with mine. "When we pick a place, we have to pick it together so we're both happy."

Evan took a rocking step back and looked up at the house again, mumbling, "Wouldn't mind a place like this. But only if I didn't have to clean it."

Luna let out a low, throaty chuckle that did things to my insides that were *not* good, given our current situation. "Yeah, well, other than this once-a-month gig we have going on, who do you think cleans this place? Speaking of, I pulled out everything you need and placed it by the front door." She pointed at the flowerbeds lining the porch. I'm going to be messing around out here so I'm not in your way." One brow went up. "I'm assuming, given you're more than old enough, I don't need to follow behind you to make sure you do a good job?"

Evan's cheeks flushed, her head lowered. "No, ma'am."

"Okay, then the clock starts now. Also, I have some Cokes in the fridge. Feel free to grab one if you want."

"Thanks." Evan lifted her hand in a wave as she glanced over her shoulder. "Bye, Dad."

"Bye, sweetheart. See you in a few hours. Love you," I called when she disappeared across the threshold, closing the door behind her with a thud.

All I heard in response was, "Uh-huh." I remembered when I'd been around her age and it stopped being cool to tell my folks I loved them or give my mom a kiss on the cheek when there were other people around. I'd never thought about Evan reaching that stage until I woke up one day and she was in it. It had crushed me then, and it still did now.

I hadn't realized I was still staring at the closed door separating me and my kid until Luna spoke. "They grow out of that phase, you know," she said, pulling me back into the present. When I looked at her, she tipped her head to where I'd been rubbing the ache in the center of my chest with the heel of my palm without realizing I was doing it. "The whole, I'm-too-cool-to-show-my-parents-affection phase. I'm sure you know that already. I went through the same thing. Only lasted a couple years."

"Same," I grunted. "Still, it hurts like hell when it happens. I wasn't prepared."

She shrugged and moved across the porch to the railing, resting her back end on it and crossing her ankles. "That means you care. That's a good thing. You know, if you're worried about leaving her here alone with me, it's a waste of your time. I wouldn't do anything to risk my chances at free labor."

I laughed, leaning back beside her and folding my arms over my chest. "I'm not worried. My folks adore you, so I know there has to be at least a little good in there. Either that, or you've got them and the whole town snowed."

Her laugh had a smoky, feminine quality to it that made my dick stir and my chest tighten. "Of course. You're the only one who sees the real, evil me."

I turned my head and arched a brow. "I knew I was extra clever."

"Mm-hmm. As a matter of fact, once Evan's done in there, I'm going to get her good and liquored up and take her for her first tattoo."

I pointed at her face and warned, "No names, and no tramp stamps."

She saluted me with a giggle. "Got it. Those are too cliché anyway. I was thinking I'd talk her into a huge back piece."

I shook my head on a chuckle. It was nice, not going for each other's jugulars and talking like regular people. Especially considering our last blowup at the office a couple days earlier, in which Luna had dressed me down so brilliantly I hadn't been able to form a response.

"I owe you an apology," I admitted, and from the

corner of my eye, I saw her head jerk around in my direction.

"Excuse me?"

"That last argument we got into at the office," I reminded. "You were right. About all of it. My attitude was out of line, and I'm sorry."

When too much time passed without a response from her, I turned and looked in her direction. Those big, warm cinnamon brown eyes of hers were wide with bewilderment. "What? Why are you staring at me like that?"

"Sorry, I never thought I'd live to see the day you admitted you were wrong about something or apologized. Then to experience both back-to-back?" she gave her head a shake as her lips tilted upward. "I thought maybe I was having a stroke."

I remembered that she could be a smartass from our night together, but I'd forgotten she could do it in a way I really fucking liked.

"All right," I said dryly, fighting back a grin. "I hope you savored the experience because it's never going to happen again."

"What? Admitting you're wrong?"

I gave her a cutting look. "Being wrong."

Her head fell back on a laugh, that fiery hair dancing around her shoulders and back. The breeze picked up, blowing past us and stirring those long locks, sending that arousing scent of hers right into my face. I had to get out of there before I made a fool of myself and tented my pants like a fucking kid. "All right, I guess I'll go. Have her call me when she's done, and I'll come get her. If you need me, you have my number. I'll be in the office catching up on some work."

She turned, her gaze trailing me as I descended the porch steps. "You're going in to work? On a Saturday? Can't you think of anything better to do?"

"Like what?"

"Oh, I don't know. *Anything*?" she lifted her arms to her sides. "Go hang with your buddies, have a couple beers, watch sports and scratch yourself. Whatever guys do when women aren't around."

I lifted a finger, "First, that's not what guys do when there are no women around." At her arched look I added, "Okay, it's not *only* what men do when there are no women around. Second, I don't have any 'buds'," I said, using finger quotes on the last word. In case you haven't noticed, I'm new in town and have been pretty busy trying to set up a whole new life."

She folded her arms in front of her and rested them on the railing, leaning forward just enough to give me the smallest view of the cleavage she was sporting beneath her shirt. Jesus, she really was beautiful. "That's just sad, boss. And that's what you should be doing instead of going into the office; you should go make some friends." She waggled her brows playfully. "Want me to make you a playdate?"

"Goodbye, Luna." I started back toward my car, choking back a laugh the whole way. "Try not to corrupt my kid too much, yeah?"

"I make no promises," she called after me. "I was thinking we'd binge on a ton of junk food, then go swimming *before* the thirty minutes you're supposed to wait. Like rebels."

I couldn't fight back the laugh any longer.

And this is why I didn't want to hire her in the first goddamn place, I told myself as I started my car and threw it in reverse. Because now I wanted to fuck the hell out of my assistant.

Talk about a sexual harassment suit just waiting to happen.

Eighteen

LUNA

WHILE EVAN WORKED INSIDE, I'd decided to tend to the small vegetable garden I'd planted a few years back when I'd first bought the house. I'd opted for raised cedar beds and was thrilled with how well everything had taken off. Now, less than a handful of years later, I had rosemary, thyme, a variety of peppers, tomatoes, carrots, and mint, and had plans to expand so I could start growing my own lettuce and root vegetables.

I picked what was ripe, placing it in the basket beside me, and tended to the plants as the narrator trilled in my ear, about to describe—hopefully in detail—how the heroine was about to give in to the tall, bearded, grumpy hero. The cadence of the narrator's voice had dropped, going slightly breathy as the good part grew closer, when a tap on the shoulder pulled me out of the story and back to reality.

Pulling out my earbuds, I twisted and lifted my hand to shield my eyes from the sun as I looked up to see Evan standing behind me. "Hey, what's up?"

"Um, sorry to interrupt. I just wanted—Oh, hey. I've read that book," she said, pointing to the screen of my cellphone that was sitting, face up, on the ground beside me. "It's really good. Book two is even better, though."

I lifted my brows, a smile curling the edges of my lips. "Your dad know you read books like that?"

She blushed, her pale skin glowing a pretty pink. "No. He doesn't really ask about the books I read. I think he's just happy I'm reading voluntarily."

My head fell back on a laugh. "In that case, maybe we should swap suggestions."

I could have sworn her eyes lit up, but it was a little difficult to tell, thanks to the makeup. "Yeah, cool. I just wanted to tell you I'm finished inside."

My eyes widened beneath my sunglasses. "Already? It's only been—" I looked at my watch and realized time had seriously gotten away from me. "Oh, wow. Four hours. I didn't realize it had been that long."

"Yeah, you seemed really into what you're doing over here."

"That happens when I garden. Never fails. I learned to

start wearing sunscreen and big floppy hats because I'd get lost in what I was doing, and before I knew it, my skin had fried like bacon."

She wrang her hands in front of her, shifting from foot to foot. "If you want, you can go in and check before I text my dad. You know, make sure it's good enough."

I sat back on my haunches and dusted my hands together to shake some of the loose soil off my gardening gloves before pulling them off. "Well, Evan, how do you think you did?"

The fidgeting stopped, but it was obvious she was still nervous around me after what she'd done to my car. I was okay with that, it meant she knew she'd done wrong. That was the first and most crucial step. Hopefully she'd come out of this whole lesson better off.

"I did my best, I promise. I even got down on the ground and scrubbed around the toilets really good."

I let out a little laugh, finding her earnestness in that moment kind of adorable. "Okay then. I'll trust that when I walk in later, everything will look nice and clean. I don't think I need to scrutinize your work while you're still here."

Her eyes grew round with shock. "For real?"

"For real," I said with an easy shrug.

She let out a little laugh that sounded like wind chimes, and I sat and watched as she glanced around. "I thought your house was really pretty when we first drove up, but it's just as pretty out here." She took in my gardens slowly, everything from the foundation shrubs to the potted succulents to the weeping redbud. "It's like something out of a fantasy book. I could never do anything like this."

"Sure, you could. It's not as hard as it may seem. All it takes is a little knowledge and follow-through. Plants are living things, just like us. That means they need regular care. They have to eat and drink just like us. Ignore them, and they die."

She looked at the bed I was currently working in. "I always thought it would be cool to grow our own food, or at least the herbs to cook with." Her smile started a bit timid but continued to grow as she spoke. "Just step out on your back porch and pluck everything you need to flavor your chicken or whatever."

Okay, so maybe Georgia was right about this girl after all. How she spoke about gardening was something after my own heart, and before I realized I was thinking it, I said, "If you're serious about learning, I'm more than happy to teach you."

"Really?" She didn't bother masking her excitement, and I warmed to her even more.

"Sure. It's still early in the day and I've got a good bit more to do out here. If you want your first lesson, I'm happy to start now. Just text your dad and see if he's cool with it. If he says yes, I've got some extra gloves in the gardening shed out back."

"Okay, yeah." Her face split into a wide grin. "Cool! I'll go text him now."

"Press the soil around the base to pack it in, but not too hard. You don't want to damage the roots or accidentally break the plant."

The tip of Evan's tongue peeked out the corner of her mouth as she concentrated on her task. "Like this?"

I leaned in to inspect the small starter tomato plant she'd just planted in a pot I'd given her to take home. "Exactly. That's perfect." With an encouraging grin, I bumped her arm with my elbow. "See? I told you you could do it. You're a natural."

She looked at the plant nervously before turning back to me. "Are you sure I shouldn't keep it here with you? What if I do something wrong? I don't want to accidentally kill it."

I placed a calming hand on her forearm. "You've got this. Just remember, this little guy likes to be warm, so keep him out on your balcony. Water him once before you go to school, then check the soil when you get home.

Depending on how hot it is outside, it might need a little more. But if you ever have any questions or think something's wrong, you can always call me."

She sat back, resting her behind on her heels as she wiped at her face with the back of her gloved hand, getting a little streak of dirt on her forehead. "I don't get it."

My forehead puckered in confusion. "Don't get what, sweetie?"

"That. Right there." She pointed right at my face. "You're being so nice to me. Why?"

I shrugged and looked back at the succulent I'd potted in a cute earthenware pot—another gift for Evan to take home. "I don't know what to tell you other than I'm just a nice person. There's really not much else to it."

"You should hate me," she informed me. "After what I did, you shouldn't be able to stand me."

"You're a kid, Evan. Kids make mistakes. Tell me something. Are you a good person?"

"I-I think so."

I pursed my lips to the side and gave her a look. "Pretty sure that's something you know for sure, one way or another."

"Then . . . Yeah. I'm a good person."

I nodded in agreement. "I know. And I know because every time you've seen me since you keyed the living hell out of my car, you've either looked close to tears, terrified, or ashamed. A bad person wouldn't care. The fact that you do speaks volumes. You could have shown up here full of that attitude I've witnessed, but even though you were here to do something I'm sure you had no desire to do, you didn't. You were polite and respectful, and you accepted your punishment." I reached up and swiped at that dirt on her face. "You're a good person, Evan. You just did something stupid. It happens to the best of us."

She looked down at her lap, her expression falling with shame. "I've been doing a lot of that lately," she admitted quietly, her voice so small it could have been carried off on a breeze. "That's why we're here in the first place."

"Hey." I bumped into her so she'd look at me. "Here's not such a bad place to be. You give it a chance, you might realize what everyone who lives here already knows. Whitecap is an awesome place to live. Cut yourself a little slack, yeah? You're young, and your life's in a bit of an upheaval at the moment. You'll find your way back to you."

She patted at the dirt around her tomato plant a little more. "Just so you know, I don't really want my dad to get back with my mom. So if you want to like, date him or something, I might be okay with that."

"Oh, honey. Your dad and I, we aren't—"

"He wasn't happy when he was with her," she spat out quickly. "I know that. I'm not stupid. I could see he was miserable. She was always complaining about something. Always griping to him, like he couldn't do anything right. I was scared he wouldn't want me anymore either."

It felt like someone had just reached into my chest and squeezed my heart. I wanted to lean over and wrap her up in the biggest, tightest hug. The only thing stopping me from doing it was that it didn't feel right, not yet. Today had been a good day, but we were still getting to know each other. Sure, she was opening up to me, but sometimes it was easier to vent your frustrations to a quasi-stranger than someone you knew.

"Why would you think that?"

She shrugged. "Just . . . some stuff my mom said."

I sat silently, waiting to see if she'd say more. When she didn't, I let out a breath and told her, "If there comes a day where you feel like sharing with me what your mom said to you, I'm here. If that day never comes, that's fine too. But I have to tell you, honey, if she said something that made you think, even for a second, that your dad wouldn't want you, wouldn't move heaven or earth for you—and I know he would because I see it in his face when he looks at you— she's dead wrong."

"I'm not his real daughter."

Georgia had told me she said that, she felt that, but I hadn't been prepared to hear it, not the way she said it just then. She wasn't being snotty or obstinate. She wasn't trying to be hurtful. As she said those words, she sounded . . . sad. Broken. Like just the possibility they could be true crushed her entire world.

She sniffled and wiped at her nose with the back of her hand, staring down at the baby tomato plant like it was the most fascinating thing on the planet.

The sadness on her face was just too much. Scooting off my haunches, I shifted on the grass so I was facing her, crossing my legs and pulling them close to me. "Can I tell you something?"

"Sure."

"My dad hasn't been in the picture since . . . well, forever, really. He left when I was so young, I don't even remember what he looks like. My mom wasn't much better. Sure, she stuck around physically, but she never had time for me. She was always chasing one relationship after another. I came in a distant second to every single one of those guys, and let me tell you, they were *not* a pack of winners."

She let out a little giggle before slapping a hand over her mouth. "Sorry. I didn't mean to laugh."

I waved her off. "It's fine. The point I'm trying to make is I know what it feels like when your own parent doesn't want you, and I know my own parents never did a single thing to try and help me like your dad has done for you. Your grandmother is more of a mom to me than my own. Same with your grandpa. Blood doesn't always matter, honey. Sometimes, the best family you could ask for is the one you choose, not the one you're born into." I tapped the center of her chest. "Your dad chose you. From where I'm sitting, I can see why, and you can believe me because I say that *after* you keyed my car."

On that one, we both giggled.

Nineteen

NATE

WHEN I'D PICKED up Evan from Luna's earlier that day, there had been a noticeable difference. For the first time in a long time, Evan actually seemed . . . happy. I saw sparks of the laughing, joking girl I'd missed like I would my own arm. Despite the fact that she still had a few more days left on her sentence, I'd decided to ride that high and swing by Rizzoli's for a couple pizzas and take them over to my parents' for an impromptu family dinner. Evan had been all for the idea, even got excited, a nice change of pace from the moody teen I'd been dealing with for what felt like an eternity.

She and my mom had spent the majority of the evening in the kitchen, with my daughter learning to bake from the master, while Dad and I hung in the living room with his cooler of beers. When it came time to leave, Mom and Evan were still at it, so when she'd asked if she could spend the night—and of course my mother teamed up with her—I hadn't been able to say no.

I left by myself, turning my car toward our tiny apartment, when Luna's words from earlier about getting out and making friends popped into my head. Truth was, even though it was the first time in months I could have gone home to an empty house and basked in the peace and quiet, I didn't want to. As sad as it was to admit, it wasn't just the move back to Whitecap that had put a damper on my social life. Even in San Francisco, I hadn't had many friends. To avoid my bad marriage, I'd buried myself in work until there wasn't much time for anything else.

Hell, the last time I'd been out was the night I met Luna, and even then, it had been more to wallow in a few beers about the sad state of my life than to kick back and relax. I was a forty-year-old divorced single father. Luna had been right. I needed to get a fucking life. That was why, instead of going back to our tiny, uncomfortable apartment, I'd changed directions on a whim.

I could hear the music, feel the pump of the bass in my chest, before I opened the door to Dropped Anchor, Whitecap's local watering hole. I'd driven by it nearly every evening when I left the office, and there were always a decent number of cars in the parking lot.

I hadn't been inside yet, but the walk from my car to

the entrance was enough for me to tell this place was a far sight better than the shithole I'd met Luna in some months back.

I pulled the door open and stepped in, surprised to see the place was bigger than I had initially thought. The wide, U-shaped bar dominated the back wall, directly across from the entrance. The old, scarred, wooden bar top was ringed with round stools. The left side of the large space housed an orderly row of pool tables, a juke box, and a few dartboards with a scattering of high-top tables. The right held the majority of the seating: tables and booths; against the far wall, a small dance floor and stage showcased a live band, currently playing a cover of Bob Seger's "Night Moves" and doing a pretty damn good job of it.

Shuffling my way through the crowd, I bellied up to the bar and settled in on one of the empty stools.

The bartender, a woman in her mid-to-late forties if I had to guess, with dark hair and surprisingly cut arms shown off by the tank top sporting the bar's name that she was wearing, stopped in front of me. "What can I get you, sugar?"

"Beer. Whatever you have on tap. I'm not picky."

She gave me a friendly wink and knocked her knuckles against the scarred wood. "My favorite kind of customer. Be right back with that."

With the size of the crowd, I'd expected a bit of a wait

but was pleasantly surprised when she came back, setting a beer in front of me, barely a minute later. "You paying up front or starting a tab, honey?"

I wasn't sure what made me do a scan of the bar before I answered, but my eyes drifted toward the stage just as the song ended, and I spotted a familiar wave of fiery red hair moving off the dance floor like autumn leaves blowing in the wind.

I spoke without thinking. "You know what? I'll start a tab." Shifting onto one hip, I pulled my wallet out of my back pocket and passed the woman my credit card. "Thanks."

"You got it."

Lifting my beer to my lips, I took a pull as I turned back toward the stage, easily spotting that mass of silky red hair in the crowd and tracking her to a table filled with her friends. I recognized Monica and the other woman she was with, the one who worked part-time at my parents' store, Cheyanne I thought, and could only assume the two men sitting down were their significant others.

I wasn't sure if it was coincidence or because she felt me staring, but those tawny eyes came up and scanned for a moment before landing on me, right there in the middle of a crowded bar.

Even from a distance, there was no missing the surprise on her face at the sight of me before she lifted her hand in a small wave. I lifted my beer in salute, feeling a tightening in my groin at the smile that tugged at her beautiful face, and before I could think better of it, I pushed off the stool and started in her direction.

I should have stopped. I should have turned right back around and left her the hell alone. But I didn't. I closed in and leaned down to be heard over the song the band had just started up. The Stones "Gimme Shelter" this time. "Hey."

Her smile stretched wider as she looked up at me. "Hey, back. I'm surprised to see you here."

I returned her grin with one of my own. "I've got this really pushy assistant getting on my case about finding a life outside work."

"She sounds incredibly smart. You should listen to everything she says."

"She's had a couple good ideas here and there. Enough to keep me from firing her."

Her laugh sounded musical and smoky, a throaty sexiness to it that set my blood on fire. "Well, since you're here, why don't you join us?" She waved to indicate the table.

"I don't want to intrude."

She placed her hand on my arm, and I could have sworn I felt the skin heat beneath her palm. "Don't be ridiculous." Before I could object again, she addressed the table as a whole. "Guys, this is Nate. My boss and

Georgia and Dezzy's son. Nate, you remember Cheyanne, right?"

Relieved I'd remembered her name correctly, I nodded. "Yeah. Nice to see you again."

"You too," she returned politely.

"And I know Monica, from childhood," I said, giving her a wave.

"Glad you're here," she offered before leaning her head on the broad, beefy shoulder of the man beside her. "This is my husband, Sam." The retired football player, I recalled. And I could definitely see it, given his size.

"Good to meet you."

"You too," he returned.

"And that's Trey. Cheyanne's very-soon-to-be husband." Luna added, pointing to the man tucked in close beside Cheyanne, holding her to him like she was the most precious thing in the room.

"Nice to meet you. Thanks for letting me crash your evening," I said as I lowered myself into the empty seat beside Luna.

"Not a problem," Sam said. "The more the merrier. I was just about to get us another round. You good?"

I lifted my pint glass, still three-quarters full. "I'm good, thanks. But next round's on me."

He nodded and stood up, his height even more of a shock now that I could see all of it.

"Yeah, he's a pretty big dude," Luna leaned in to say, clearly having read the shock on my face. "You eventually get used to it and then he just becomes Sam: the friend you can always count on to get things from the high shelves."

I drank down more of my beer as I took in the bar, the mass of people, the band. "This place is pretty cool." I looked back to Luna with raised brows. "Definitely a step up from the last bar I saw you in."

She let out another throaty laugh, and it was the kind of sound that made a man think of sex, burying himself as deep inside a woman as he can in an effort to pull that sound from her chest. "Yeah, but then again, pretty much everything is a step up from that place." She took a drink from the beer bottle in front of her, and I might have stared longer than necessary at the way her throat worked on a swallow. "I take it being here means you have a night off from parent duty?"

"Yeah, unexpectedly. Impromptu sleepover at the grandparents. I was heading home when I remembered you giving me shit about not having a life. Figured I could at least stop in for a beer." I tilted my head toward the stage. "Didn't realize they had live music."

"Yeah. A couple Fridays and Saturdays out of the month. Just a local band, but they're great."

The dance floor wasn't exactly big, but it was jam-packed with writhing bodies. "That they are." I turned back to Luna, staying close so we could continue our conversation over the music. With mere inches between us, I could smell that tantalizing scent coming off her skin, see the small flecks of gold in her tawny eyes that made them sparkle. If I'd been smart, I would have sat up straight, put some distance between us, but I was quickly discovering that smart flew out the window when it came to this woman.

"I'm not sure what you said to Evan while you two were together today, but whatever it was, thank you. She was in a much better mood this evening than she's been in for quite some time."

"Nothing to thank me for. She's a great kid, Nate." Something about hearing that, especially from her, lifted a weight that had been sitting on my chest for far too long. She leaned even closer, placing her hand on my knee in a gesture that was meant to be comforting, but had my blood rushing all the same. Christ, how pathetic was it that such a simple, friendly touch from this woman revved my motor like she'd just reached into my pants and wrapped her fingers around my dick?

The song changed just then, and a sharp shriek of excitement wrenched through the air as Monica and Cheyanne shot to their feet. "I *love* this song! Let's, dance, Lu!" Monica demanded, grabbing Luna's hand and giving it a tug.

Luna looked at me with a small grin as her friends dragged her out of her chair. "Guess I'm dancing."

"Guess so."

Something flashed across her face just then, something that got my blood pumping even faster as she kept her eyes on me. "You'll be here when I get back?"

The expectancy in her voice damn near did me in. "I'm not going anywhere." Even though I knew I should.

Shooting me one last smile, she let the ladies drag her off to dance.

Twenty

LUNA

IF YOU HAD TOLD me a week ago I would have spent my Saturday night having a blast with Nate Warren, I'd have called you a dirty liar. But that was exactly what had happened. I wasn't sure when the hell he'd gone from being my perfect enemy to a man I enjoyed spending time with, but it was the truth . . . surprisingly.

One hour bled into the next, and between dancing and a couple more drinks, I spent the majority of the night huddled at the end of the table with Nate, talking and laughing. He blended surprisingly well with my little ragtag crew of friends, hitting it off with Sam and Trent easily and winning Cheyanne and Monica over by buying two rounds for the table.

I'd been having such a good time that I hadn't realized how late it was until Cheyanne leaned into me and tapped me on the shoulder. "Hey, sweetie. We're heading out. We need to relieve the babysitter, or she's going to start inflating her prices on us."

"Oh. Okay." My stomach sank, disappointment clawing at me as I turned back to Nate. "Sorry. I rode with them so . . ."

I could have sworn I saw a flash of want in his eyes as he quickly offered, "I can give you a ride home if you want to stay."

I jumped to accept his offer just as fast as he made it, that sinking feeling in the pit of my stomach instantly lightening until I was nice and floaty with excitement. "Yeah, sure. That's sounds good. I'm going to hang a bit longer," I told Cheyanne. "Nate will drive me home later."

The smile she gave me was smug and knowing, just condescending enough to make me want to smack her in the face. "You're sure?" she asked, that grin growing in size as I narrowed my eyes at her.

"I'm positive," I said with a growl. "Thanks, bye." I didn't miss the giggle she let out before leaning in to give me a hug. Trent did the same, reminding me to be safe before grabbing his woman and guiding her toward the exit. Sam and Monica weren't far behind, heading home themselves only a few minutes later, leaving Nate and me alone.

. . .

I had a sudden rush of déjà vu, my mind going back to that first night. I didn't do repeats, as a hard and fast rule. Once I'd been with a man, that was it. I moved on. But there was something about him, something that wouldn't let go. The smart thing would have been to leave with Cheyenne and Trent, go home, and go about my life as usual. But I wasn't feeling particularly smart right then.

The club was packed, bodies all around us. But when Nate moved his chair closer it felt like he was closing us in our own personal bubble. The sound and noises from the bar became muffled. The song the band was playing was only faint background noise as the world closed in until it was just the two of us.

"You didn't have to stay, if you didn't want to," he started. "If you're ready to go home, I can—"

I cut him off with the shake of my head. "I want to stay."

Those grayish-blue eyes sparkled as his full lips curved into a grin that made my skin tingle. "Good," he said, shifting even closer, closing more of the distance between us. "I didn't want you to leave either."

I let out a heavy sigh, giving my head a shake. It felt fuzzy; not from the alcohol, but from him. That leather and cloves scent overwhelmed my senses as I inhaled deeply. *God,* he smelled so damn good. "This isn't smart." I wasn't sure who I was trying to warn, me or him. "I'm pretty sure we both know that."

He lifted his beer to his lips, drinking back nearly half in a few gulps. Fog rolled over those eyes, making them look downright stormy. "And I'm pretty sure we're past that."

Everything in my body clenched tight. Warning sirens blared in my head, telling me I was dangerously close to breaking every single one of my rules with this guy.

Heat boiled in my veins, beneath my skin, and I sucked back my own beer in an effort to tamp it down.

Desperate to get control of the moment, I spit out the first thing that popped into my head. "What happened with you and your ex-wife?" Nate rocked back in his chair, just as surprised by my question as I was. "I'm sorry. I'm sorry; it's none of my business. I shouldn't have—"

"No, it's fine. I don't mind talking about it. I was just a bit thrown off. Kind of felt like that came out of left field."

It had, but that was what desperation did to a person.

"I've heard a bit," I hedged. "Georgia told me about the adoption, and Evan mentioned it again today."

He let out a sigh, and I could practically see the weight falling onto his shoulders. "Let me guess. She's not my *real* daughter. Christ." He grunted, reaching up to massage the space between his eyebrows.

"Well, sort of. But I got the impression that maybe her

mother had said something to make her feel that way." His expression turned to thunder, and I quickly scrambled to try and ease his rising fury. "She didn't spell it out for me, and I didn't push. But by the end of our talk, I think she was feeling a whole lot better."

"Really?"

I nodded, smiling at the hopefulness in his voice. I hadn't thought the word "cute" would be fitting for a man like Nate, but in that moment, that was exactly how he looked: cute. "Yeah, she really did. I told her sometimes the best family isn't necessarily the one you're born into, but the one you choose."

"That's the damn truth," he murmured around the rim of his glass before taking another sip, this one much smaller than the last. "I picked Evan the moment I first laid eyes on her."

I propped an elbow on the table and rested my chin in my hands. "Tell me about that," I prompted. I'd heard from Georgia already, but I wanted the story straight from his mouth. I wanted to see the emotion dance in his eyes. I wanted to hear the passion in his voice.

And he didn't disappoint. "I knew the minute I saw that little girl, she was going to be my whole world." My heart pitched in my chest, but I somehow managed to keep my composure as he continued. "I'd only been dating Amber, her mom, for a couple months when I first met her. She'd been playing in the backyard and had been covered in dirt. Her hair hung halfway down her back and was a tangled mess of leaves and twigs from where she'd been rolling around in the grass." He smiled adoringly at the memory, making my belly flutter. "She was barely two feet tall and looked up at me with these huge blue eyes that took up half her face. She looked like a little dirt-smudged doll, and the first thing she said to me was "Giant!" and that was it. That was all it took for her to steal my heart, and I never got it back."

Oh God, I thought. *I've just made a huge mistake.* That story, the look on his face as he told it, it did . . . things . . . to me. Made me feel things I'd told myself I would *never* feel for a man.

"You want the truth about my ex?"

I nodded, unable to speak since my mouth had gone dry.

"The truth is, if not for Evan, that relationship wouldn't have gone much further than it already had. Hell, I was already thinking about ending it. I didn't want to marry her. I didn't love her the way a man should love a woman he was going to pledge his life to, but it was the only way I could keep Evan in my life. Amber was always using her daughter as a pawn in our relationship because she knew that. I agreed to marry her because she told me if

I wasn't willing to take the next step, there was no point in us staying together."

My heart twisted. "And you'd lose Evan."

"I had no claim over her. I wasn't even her stepdad. But I don't regret it. Not for a goddamn second. Amber thought she was clever, playing her games. But I played one of my own. The ink was barely dry on our marriage certificate. She was riding the high of being married to a man who was well off, financially, so I took advantage of the good mood she was in because she thought she'd won, and got her to agree to let me adopt Evan. Being her stepdad wasn't enough. If we ever divorced, I'd have no rights. But I was going to make damn sure I stayed in that girl's life. She needed me."

I frowned, dread sitting like a lead ball in the pit of my stomach. "What do you mean?"

Her let out a weary sigh, drank more beer. "Evan was always more of a game piece than a daughter to Amber. She'd never planned on having kids, wasn't exactly maternally inclined, but she was careless and became pregnant. She wasn't sure who the father was, so she was going it alone, doing a job she didn't want to do in the first damn place. When she wasn't using Evan as a game piece, she was simply an inconvenience."

"I don't know this woman, never met her in my life, and I know I've only spent a small amount of time with your daughter, but I kind of want to find this Amber and punch her in the face."

Nate's chuckle was a mixture of humor and sadness. "Believe me, I understand how you feel. I lived it for too many years. When I finally couldn't take it anymore and told her I was leaving, she did everything she could to make my life hell. She dragged the divorce out, fought the custody arrangements, fought for child support. She even tried to keep Evan from me, tried claiming the adoption wasn't legal. It was pointless in the end, and a waste of money for her. It took a year, but I was finally rid of her and had joint custody of Evan. I thought, that was it. The nightmare was over. Things could finally be good. Then Evan started acting out. She was getting into so much trouble, Amber finally decided she'd had enough. Dealing with her own daughter was too much of an inconvenience, and since she wasn't really big on those, she all but dropped her on my doorstep, said she couldn't handle it anymore."

"Oh God. Poor Evan."

He nodded sadly. "I told her, if she did this, there was no going back. She had to sign full custody over to me."

"What did she say to that?"

His laugh was bitter, full of hatred. "She couldn't sign the new custody agreement fast enough, basically gave up any and all rights to her own damn kid."

The longer he spoke, the more the puzzle pieces fell into place. One after the other, clicking into their slots until the picture became clear as day. Evan wasn't acting out just for the hell of it.

"God, Nate. I'm so sorry."

"Not your fault. You weren't a terrible mother."

No, I wasn't. But like Evan, I knew all too well how it felt to have a shitty mother. And knowing what I knew now only endeared the girl to me that much more. "It sucks that her mom is a bitch, but you have to know, she's going to be all right."

He sighed again, and I practically felt the weight of it. "Doesn't seem that way sometimes."

"Maybe not, but she will. Trust me. I could see it in her today. This whole thing, the divorce and her mom, made it hard for her to trust that things are going turn out okay. Give her time and she'll see you're going to stick. That's all she needs. And something tells me, she's already started coming around."

He studied me intensely, his face so close he was all I could see, those eyes swirling like a turbulent sea on a stormy day. "Fuck," he breathed, dropping his head and repeating more passionately, "*Fuck!*"

"What?" I asked in a panic, reaching out to place my hand on top of his. "What's wrong?"

"I knew it." He gave his head a defeated shake. "I knew

this was going to happen." When he looked back up, trapping my gaze with his, nearly all the air expelled from my lungs. "I knew once wasn't going to be enough. Not with you."

"Nate," I whispered, trying to stop my head from spinning. "We can't—"

"Tell me you don't feel it, Luna. Tell me I'm the only one with this fucking *need*, and I'll let it go. I'll leave it alone and won't ever mention it again."

I couldn't say that because it would have been a bald-faced lie. "It's not that simple. I want you, I do," I confessed, sending my heart rate through the roof. "But you're my boss. And I don't do relationships." I could barely hear myself speak, hear myself think, over the blood rushing in my ears. "It's a disaster waiting to happen."

"Probably."

I pulled in a deep breath, shoring up my nerves. "But . . ." I started, unable to stop myself. "Maybe, if it's just this one last time." His eyes lit up like a kid in a candy store. "And there are no strings—" He shot out of his chair, quick as lightning. "Wait, what are you doing?"

"I'm not giving you a chance to change your mind. We're going. Now. Your place or mine?"

I guess that settled it. "Mine's closer."

Twenty-One

LUNA

THE VOICE in the back of my head, telling me I was making a huge mistake, had given up about thirty seconds after I followed Nate out of the bar when it became obvious I wasn't going to listen.

We left the bar without touching, there would be no hand-holding or anything of the sort to get tongues wagging, but as soon as we made it to his car, something in Nate snapped. He beeped the locks, but before I could get the passenger door open, he grabbed my arm and spun me around, using his body to force mine back against the car. With his front plastered to mine, he lowered his head and took my mouth with his. The kiss wasn't fierce and rushed, but it wasn't calm and sedate either. It was potent and intoxicating. He easily parted my lips with his and slid his tongue inside to gently stroke against mine. The feel of it made my knees tremble, and I would have slid right down onto the asphalt had he not been holding me up.

When he pulled back—all too soon—we were both breathing heavily. I blinked to clear the sudden fuzziness from my vision and tilted my head up to see him staring down at me with a look I could only describe as primal. "Let's go." He finally backed up enough to give me room to move, holding on to my elbow as he opened the door and guided me into the seat.

He broke several traffic laws on the way to my house, but I never once felt unsafe. If anything, his need for me was so great that going seven miles over the speed limit only turned me on that much more.

Crushed shell spit back from his tires as he whipped into my driveway and jerked to an abrupt stop, and within seconds, he had me by the hand and was pulling me up the front steps.

"Damn, this really is some view," he said once we were inside. I hadn't turned on any interior lights, so the full moon reflecting off the water poured into my living room from the big picture windows on the back of the house, bathing everything in soft, blue-tinged light. "And this is some house."

"You want a tour?" I curled my lips between my teeth and bit down to stifle my giggle at the look he gave me just then. "Okay, no tour."

"Tour later. Right now I need inside you."

Shifting to stand in front of him, I dragged my fingernail down the front of my shirt as I lifted on my tiptoes, my lips whispering against his as I said, "If you like this view, you should see the one from my bedroom."

I let out a sharp yelp of surprise that morphed into a full belly laugh when, with an animal-like growl, he lifted me right off the ground and started for the stairs. I happily wrapped my legs around his waist as he carried up like I weighed no more than air. Burying my face in his neck, I inhaled deeply, taking his scent into my lungs and holding it for as long as I could.

"God, you always smell so good. I think I'm addicted to your scent."

His fingers clenched my ass, the pressure nearly enough to leave bruises, but I didn't mind one damn bit. "I know I'm addicted to yours. Which way?"

"Right. There's only one door. That's my room."

A second later, he carried me past the threshold into my bedroom. Sure enough, the view was breathtaking. Enough so that he had to stop and take it in. "Holy shit. You weren't lying, baby."

My back wall consisted mainly of windows, and with the blinds drawn and the curtains open, the room practically glowed. The inky midnight sky was speckled with millions of white stars, and the moon was so big it almost seemed like you could reach out and touch it. The white-caps glimmered off the top of the waves.

"I fell in love with this house the moment I saw it. I dreamed of living here for longer than I can remember. I stepped inside, and that love was solidified. But this view was why I put an offer in on a house I couldn't afford. As soon as I saw it, I knew I was home."

"I can see why." Then, just like that, his fascination with the view disappeared, and his focus turned solely on me.

I couldn't remember a time in my life when I'd wanted anything as much as I wanted him.

When his lips came back to mine, I wrapped my arms around him, dragging my nails down his back and fisting the material of his shirt. He kissed me like he was born to do it, like it was the reason he existed. His mouth formed perfectly to mine, like they were made for each other.

My head fell back on a groan when he broke from my lips to lick down my neck. "You're wearing too many clothes," I argued, yanking at his shirt again.

He took me by the arms and shifted me back a few inches, looking at me as a raspy chuckle scraped up his throat. Then, like some sort of sexual ninja magician, he had us both stripped down to nothing in the blink of an eye.

Cupping one of my swollen breasts in his large hand,

he lashed at my aching nipple with his tongue before scraping it with the stubble on his chin. "That better?"

I let out a pathetic whimper as I fisted his hair. "Worse. You're going to tease me to death."

One second, I was on my feet, the next I was falling backward into the fluff of my cozy white comforter. "Oh, no, Luna." The smile that stretched across his lips had me clenching my thighs as liquid warmth pooled in my belly. "I'd never tease you to death. My goal is death by orgasm."

As if to prove his point, he spread my legs wide, holding them open with his palms on the insides of my thighs, as he dragged his wicked tongue up my center.

I cried out, arching off the bed as he buried his face between my legs. The flutter in my core matched the flutter of his tongue as he flicked and teased that tiny bundle of nerves before driving his tongue inside me. He had me writhing on the bed in no time, fisting the comforter so tight I thought I might rip it as my hips undulated, rubbing at his face.

I came just like that, on his tongue, in his mouth, until I saw stars on the backs of my eyelids and my throat was raw from crying out his name.

He had a Cheshire cat grin firmly in place when he crawled up my body, grabbing me behind the knees and wrapping my legs around his hips. "That's one."

Oh God, he really *was* going to try and make me

climax to death. "Nate, I don't think—*oh my God*," I finished on a shout as he plunged into me, his thick cock stretching me wide. I could feel him *everywhere*.

"Sorry, what were you saying?"

I opened my eyes and glared even though I was sure the glassiness of my gaze dulled the menace. "Shut up and move," I ordered, reached down to grab hold of his ass so I could pull him closer, deeper. "God, you feel so good."

He pulled out of me and slid back in, over and over, his rhythm and strength increasing with every inward glide. "Jesus, you're fucking beautiful like this." He lifted one hand from where it was braced on the mattress and brushed back a lock of hair that had fallen across my forehead. "Your skin glows like moonbeams in this light."

A sound akin to a sob broke in my throat. The coil inside me tightening, his sweet words as he looked down at me while moving inside me. My chest suddenly felt tight. Everything felt tight.

"Nate," I said on a breath.

"You're beautiful, Luna. You *feel* beautiful."

I broke at his tenderness. My eyes rolled back, my neck arched, and every muscle in my body strained as the release washed through me, over me, threatening to pull me under.

"That's it. *Christ,* just like that," Nate coaxed, picking up his pace. "If you saw what I see. Most stunning thing

I've ever laid eyes on when you come, baby. Let me have another."

I wasn't sure if it was another one, or if the last one just went of forever, but by the time it left me, I felt boneless. I had just enough wherewithal to focus on Nate as he buried himself deep and grunted out his own release. I could feel every twitch, every jerk of him inside me as he emptied himself. When he finished, he collapsed, burying his face in my neck.

"I'll stop crushing you in a minute," he said, his voice muffled against my skin and hair. "I need to catch my breath."

I giggled as much as I could with his weight pressing down on me. "Stay as long as you want," I assured him, locking my ankles and wrists around him loosely. "You'll get no complaints from me."

He nuzzled against my neck. "God, what's that perfume? I can't get enough of your smell."

"I don't wear perfume. It's my shampoo and conditioner. Amber Dreams or something like that."

He inhaled deeply one more time before finally rolling off me and onto his back, hooking his arm around my waist and pulling me with him so I was snuggled into his side.

He filled his lungs before letting it out with a huff. "We have a serious problem, moonbeam."

The endearment washed through me, but I pushed the gooey warmth of it away, telling myself I'd deal with it at another time. I lifted my head and cocked my brows. "Already? That was fast."

"You know that thing about this being a one-time deal and working it out of our systems?"

My heart rate kicked up and my stomach plummeted at the reminder. "Vaguely. Why?"

He shook his head with mock weariness, taking on a dramatically serious tone. "It didn't work."

"Oh my," I said softly, holding back my laughter. "That is serious."

"It really is. I'm going to need you at least . . . ten more times."

I bugged my eyes out. "Ten?"

His arm around me clenched tighter. "At least."

I pretended to think long and hard on that. "Well . . . ten is a nice, round number."

His lips creeped up in a smile that overtook his whole face and made me shiver. "I was thinking the exact same thing."

"Well then we're agreed," I said on a yawn, feeling the kind of bone-deep exhaustion that could only come with having had world-class sex. "That's a first for us. Usually we disagree on pretty much everything simply out of spite."

He stretched his free arm up and brought it around and under his head, making himself more comfortable in my bed. "I like this getting along thing. Especially when it leads to such a nice outcome. Although, I kind of liked some of the aspects that came with being enemies too." He waggled his eyebrows. "Sometimes it felt like foreplay."

I let out a snort and rolled my eyes, the moonlight bright enough so he could see it. "I'm glad one of us did, because I found it annoying as hell."

He gave me a playful shake, the motion making my nipples scrape lightly over the thin bit of hair on his chest. And just like that, my arousal shot through the roof. "Come on, admit it. You like being my enemy from time to time."

This time I actually did give that some thought instead of just pretending. "Okay," I relented grudgingly. "Maybe a *little*. But that is not carte blanche to act like an asshole."

My body shook with his as he laughed lightly. "Yes ma'am. Now get some sleep. I need you well rested. By my count, I got you off three times that last go-round, so I've got my work cut out for me."

Twenty-Two

LUNA

I SLOWLY BLINKED my eyes open against the sunshine pouring into my bedroom like a freaking spotlight. Usually I closed the shades right before bed for that very reason, but after the . . . activities the night before. I'd fallen asleep and forgotten.

Rolling over onto my back, I lifted my arms over my head and pointed my toes in a deep stretch, feeling aches in muscles that hadn't been used in quite some time and an all too pleasurable twinge between my thighs that made me smile. I reached across the mattress to the cause of those aches, but came up empty, feeling nothing but cold sheets beneath my palm, telling me he'd been gone a while.

Sitting up, I looked around for Nate, but the only sign of him was his clothes from the night before scattered around my bedroom floor. Everything but his jeans. Throwing the covers off, I snatched up his tee, bringing it to my nose and sniffing in that all-too familiar scent, then slipped it over my head before padding out of the room on sleep-heavy feet.

I hit the landing and let out a big yawn, noticing for the first time the strong scent of coffee and the sound of waves crashing on the shore.

"Jesus. You come down those stairs sounding like a Clydesdale."

My head whipped around toward the opened sliding door that led to the back deck. That explained the noise. And Nate standing there dressed in those jeans, the button still undone and his feet bare, shoulder propped on the doorjamb as he sipped coffee from a mug, explained the smell.

"Shut up," I grumbled, rubbing the remainder of the sleep from my eyes.

His laugh, while *very* sexy, made me want to punch him in the face. "I see someone isn't a morning person." He ignored my little snarl. "And has one hell of a case of bedhead."

I couldn't be bothered to reach up and touch my hair to see how bad it was. Honestly, I didn't give a damn. I padded over to the door instead of heading for the kitchen, taking the mug right out of his hands. "Coffee," I grunted before taking a nice, long sip.

He stared down at me like I was a lunatic before smiling again and looping an arm around my waist, pulling me into him. "You know there's a full pot in your kitchen."

The instant jolt of caffeine worked wonders in making me feel more human. "That would have taken too long to cool. I needed something now."

"In that case, I'm happy to have been of service. By the way, you look fucking incredible in my shirt."

I took another sip. "Thanks. I'll keep it then. What time is it?"

"Just after eight."

I face planted against his chest, the bare skin warm from the sun. *Man*, did it feel nice when that arm he had around me squeezed and a chuckle vibrated up from deep in his belly. After our first round the night before, Nate and I had snoozed a bit, but it hadn't been long before he woke me up on the cusp of orgasm number four. Then he'd proceeded to keep me awake for a few more hours, meaning I'd had one hell of a workout and had only gotten about four hours sleep.

"How are you awake right now? I'm exhausted?" I lamented into his chest.

"Internal clock. Damn thing started up when Evan

entered my life and I haven't been able to shut it off since. Now seven thirty is considered sleeping in." At my pathetic whimper, he kissed the top of my head and began guiding me toward the kitchen. "Come on, sleepyhead. I'll make you some breakfast."

I rocked back on a heel as he continued around the island toward the coffee maker. Like he'd been there a million times, he opened a cabinet, pulled down a mug, and filled it for himself.

I lifted my free hand and gave it a wave. "Hold on a minute. You cook?"

"I do. You think I grew up in a house with Georgia Warren and somehow managed to get around cooking lessons?" He scoffed and shook his head. "No way."

I hopped onto one of the bar stools and settled in to watch. "All right then, Chef Warren. What are you making me?"

Placing his coffee cup on the counter, he moved across the space to the fridge. "Well, let's see what you've got." He opened the door and studied the confines before doing the same with the pantry.

"Wait. You can just look and build a whole meal around whatever's on hand?"

"Yep. Pretty much. And with what you have, I can do biscuits and sausage gravy or a bacon and"—he pulled out a block of cheese and read the label—"gruyere omelet." He ducked his head back into the fridge as my mouth began to water. "Would have been nice if you had some fresh thyme—"

"I do," I chirped happily, pointing back at the sliding glass door. "In my herb garden. I have fresh thyme, basil, cilantro, and rosemary. And I choose the omelet, because that sounds *divine*."

He moved back around the counter toward me, stopping to place a kiss on my forehead. "Then the omelet it is. Be right back."

Nate headed outside, and while he scoured my gardens for fresh herbs to pick for my homemade breakfast, I laid my head down on the counter, pressing my cheek into the cold quartz as I gave myself a lecture, trying to stop the freak-out brewing inside me.

This wasn't serious. This was just sex. Sure, we'd backpedaled a bit on the whole one-time deal, but that didn't mean anything. It didn't have to mean anything. We'd get this out of our system eventually, and when that happened, we could go back to how things were before—hopefully without the whole enemies part. Maybe we could even be friends when all was said and done.

"You okay?"

I shot up so fast my head spun and I nearly toppled backward off the stool. "Yep. Good. All good here. You get what you were looking for?"

He held up a batch of thyme and got busy pulling the rest of the ingredients out of the fridge. He opened cabinets and drawers until he found the utensils he was looking for and got down to work "I gotta tell you, your gardens are impressive. Evan said as much when I picked her up, but seeing them up close for myself . . . I'd give an arm for an herb and vegetable garden like that."

For some insane reason, I felt a blush creep up my skin. "Thanks. Yeah, I told Evan I'd teach her about gardening if she was interested. She seemed pretty into it."

"Hence the plants you gave her."

"Exactly." I smiled. "I hope she liked them."

He looked up from expertly chopping the thyme. "Are you kidding? She insisted the plants stay overnight at Grandma's with her because she didn't trust me to water the tomato this morning."

I let out a laugh and arched a brow. "Considering where you're standing right now, her lack of trust might have been warranted."

"Hey." He pointed the big Chef's knife in my direction. "If I'd had my grandplant with me yesterday, I never would have set foot in that bar. I would have been responsible and taken it home for a good night's rest."

I finished off my coffee and hummed. "Uh-huh. Sure you would have."

When I rolled out of bed this morning, I'd half expected things between Nate and me to be awkward. I never in a million years would have thought I'd be drinking coffee and watching a sexy-as-hell man waltz around my kitchen, shirtless, while making me a breakfast that smelled so delicious, I drooled a little bit. It was amazing how things could take such a drastic turn in such a short amount of time. Then again, the easy conversation and quick laughs were what had drawn me to him that first night.

After that job interview, I'd brushed that first encounter off as him being on his best behavior so he could get in my pants. But now I saw the truth. That first night was the real him. Outside circumstances had played a large part in us butting heads the past several weeks, but that first night had been the truth. Which was a huge fucking problem, because I could *really* start to like this guy.

On that thought, the tinny ring of my cellphone broke through my melancholy. Hopping off the stool, I moved to where I'd dropped my purse on the table near the front door. I pulled it out and felt the nice, happy morning I'd been having come to a screeching halt at the sight of my mom's name on the screen.

"Everything okay?"

I looked up and offered Nate a smile I hoped didn't

look as brittle as it felt. "Yep. Sure. I have to take this. I'll be right back."

Nate

I waited until she'd gone down the hall and entered another room before following after her. I had no right to listen in on her private conversation. I knew I was crossing a line by eavesdropping. But I also knew whoever was on the other line had taken the sparkle out of her eyes that had been there from the first moment the coffee kicked in.

Yesterday had been the first time in a couple months I'd seen more than just a glimpse of the Luna I met a couple months back. With a truce called and our weapons lowered, we'd both gone back to the people we'd been that first night. That was the Luna I'd gotten this morning as well, the one who talked and teased as she drank coffee and ogled me while I made breakfast.

Then she'd looked at her phone and her face had gone pale. The light in her eyes died, and that smile she'd given me was fake as hell. I defended my actions by telling myself I wasn't trying to be nosey. I was genuinely concerned.

The door hadn't shut all the way, and when I stopped,

off to the side and out of sight, I saw that it was set up as a home office, probably the very one she'd worked out of when she had her own business.

"Hi, Mom," she answered after bringing her phone up to her ear. "Hold on, wait. Just slow down. What's the matter?"

I moved a little closer to get a better view and saw her lower her head and reach up to rub at the space between her eyes as she listened to her mother on the other end of the call. I knew that look well; I'd experienced it more than a handful of times myself. It was exasperation and weariness all rolled into one.

"No. No, I told you, I can't help you anymore." She dropped into a cozy looking chair, leaning her head back to stare at the ceiling, as if looking for divine intervention.

"Have you already forgotten our last conversation? The one where I called *you* asking for help for the first time in my life? No. Yeah. That's right. And you said you couldn't afford it." Another pause. "Well, where's Dwight? If you need money, ask him, because I don't have it, Mom." She let out a laugh so bitter it was painful to hear. "Of course he did. Of course! Because that's the only time you call me. I don't exist until your latest boyfriend dumps you, but that's only so you can leech off me. Then, like clockwork, you meet another guy and forget I exist all over again. Well it's not happening this time."

My chest grew frigidly cold as the blood in my veins started to freeze. I'd wondered about the connection Luna had with my girl, but now it made perfect sense. Both of them were part of a sad, fucked-up club in which you had to have a shitty mother to belong.

"No, Mom. No! I'm done! Even if I could help you, I wouldn't. Consider it returning the favor for all you've done for me. Not that any of that matters because I *can't*. From now on, you're going to have to get a job when you're between boyfriends, because I can't help you."

She pulled the phone from her ear and I spun around, moving on silent feet back to the kitchen. I expected her to be in right after me, but one minute ticked into the next, then the next. So while I waited, I worked on breakfast.

Finally, five minutes later, she returned. She stopped at the stool and looked at her coffee mug before turning those cinnamon eyes to me. "You topped off my coffee?"

"Yeah," I answered casually. "I figured you're one of those people who doesn't hit one hundred until you've had at least two cups."

She sat back down and lifted the cup. "I am. Thank you."

"Not a problem."

I wanted to push. I wanted to ask what was wrong, hoping she'd open up, but I didn't. I wasn't sure it was my place. I'd have given my left arm to make her feel better, to put that gleam back in her eyes, but I'd agreed this was just sex, no strings, no complications. She'd been adamant that she didn't want a relationship.

And something told me if I broke that rule, she'd go running so fast I'd never be able to catch her.

Twenty-Three

LUNA

WITH MY HEAD held high and my shoulders back, I headed for Nate's office, determined to keep things one hundred percent professional. We were at work, after all, and the office was no place to mess around. Unless you were starring in a porno. Or your boss was *incredibly* hot. And damn it! I'd lapsed back into a big ball of horny nerves again. I could do this. I could maintain professionalism at work and keep the sexy stuff for the off-hours. After all, it had only been a day.

It had taken some time to shake the funk the call from my mother had put me in the morning before, but with hard work and determination, I'd managed to push it to the back of my mind and salvage the rest of the day.

Nate hadn't been joking when he said he could cook.

The man dominated in the kitchen. I wasn't sure I'd ever tasted anything half as good as the omelet he'd made me. He was gorgeous, built, funny, successful, an incredible father, *and* he could cook like a pro. It was almost too much. After literally scraping my plate clean, he'd ravaged me on the kitchen island before carrying me back to bed and doing the same thing all over again. He'd really put his all into the whole death by orgasm thing before he had to head home and change so he could pick Evan up from his parents' house.

It had been less than twenty-four hours since we last saw each other, but as I was getting ready for work this morning I was incredibly aware I still felt him every time I moved. I needed to keep my cool. The only way this could work was if the lines were clearly drawn. The rules were set in place and not crossed. Fun. No strings.

Keeping my tone light, I rapped my knuckles against his opened door. "Good morning. I've got your coffee."

"Ah, perfect." He stood up and rounded the desk, meeting me in front of it. Quick as lightning, he took the mug from my hands and twisted, placing it next to his computer in one graceful, smooth motion before taking my face in his hands and bringing his lips down on mine in a frenzied, passionate kiss.

I nearly succumbed to the deliciousness and talent of

his mouth before my brain reengaged. It took more strength than I realized I had *and* the act of a higher power, but I somehow managed to disengage from the kiss and break from his grip.

"Hey, whoa! No, no, no." I licked my lips, then realized my mistake when I could still taste him, and dragged the back of my hand across my mouth. "What do you think you're doing?"

"What's it look like?" He reached for me again.

"Hey, knock it off!" I yelped, smacking his hands away.

His face fell. "Damn it. Will you stop hitting me and let me touch you?"

Oh, *man* I really wanted to let him touch me. He did it so damn well, but . . . "No. *No!* We can't."

His made a face that I could only describe as a full-grown man pout. It was pathetic and adorable and hilarious all at the same time. "Why the ever-loving hell not?"

I gaped at him, my jaw hanging open. "Because we're at work," I exclaimed. "There will be no messing around at work." And I kind of hated myself for saying that out loud.

"That's a stupid rule," he groused. "I'm the boss, and as the boss, I overrule all stupid rules. Now, let me kiss you."

He reached for me again, and I had to take a huge step

back to avoid him. "Stop it!" I exclaimed with a bewildered laugh. "You can't overrule that. This is the way it has to be. Between the hours of eight and five, you're my boss and I'm your assistant, and that's all we are. Please, Nate."

At the pleading quality my voice took on by the end of that declaration, he stopped and let out a sigh, tucking his hands into his pockets. "You're really serious about this?"

"I am. If we don't keep the lines clearly in place, things could get complicated. We can't let that happen. That's not what we are. We aren't complicated. Besides, you have an appointment with Ms. Swanson in less than thirty minutes. That wouldn't leave us enough time anyway."

He all but stuck out his bottom lip as he pouted, "Would've been enough time to watch you come on my fingers."

I let out a pained groan. "God, you can't say stuff like that!"

He blew out a long, long sigh. "Fine. Fine, I'll follow your stupid rule, which makes absolutely no sense. But I'll do it, because it's important to you."

He really was battering at those walls I was trying desperately to keep up. I wanted to cave over and over, and as the day progressed, it became harder to fight off that desire. I'd never had a problem walking away from a partner before. Once it was done, that was it. The men always knew the score, so when I felt things had run their course, we'd part ways, and that was the end of it. But this . . . thing I was doing with Nate . . . it didn't feel the same. I wasn't quite sure walking away would be as easy. But despite how terrifying that thought was, I couldn't bring myself to pull the plug just yet.

God, what a mess.

I did my best to focus on my work. I answered calls, made appointments, ordered supplies that were running low. I kept busy so I wouldn't think about Nate and how much I wanted him. There was only one tiny problem: he was always *there*. His smell, the sound of his voice; there was no escaping it while I was at work.

He'd stayed true to his word and backed off, doing his best to stay in his office and not intrude on my space, but it was no use. Even if he wasn't around, I was still *thinking* about him. Hell, I couldn't seem to take my mind off him.

It was enough to drive me insane. By the time my lunch break rolled around, I was at the end of an extremely frayed rope and highly agitated, which put me in a downright pissy mood.

Snatching my purse up, I hooked the strap on my shoulder and stood from my desk, stomping on my heels to his doorway, arms crossed, face full of attitude.

It took him a second to realize I was standing there,

but when he lifted his gaze from his computer screen, giving me those misty gray eyes, I felt a flutter in my core.

"Hi," he said pleasantly, his smile warm and happy.

Damn it.

"I'm going to lunch," I snapped, crossing my arms over my chest. It was completely irrational, but I couldn't help myself. There was nothing rational about how I felt when it came to that man.

He was the picture of calm as he leaned back in his chair, interlocking his fingers and resting his palms on his flat stomach. "Everything all right?"

"Yep," I snapped, the sexual frustration bubbling inside of me like lava. "Everything's just dandy. I'll be back when I'm back."

With that, I whipped around and started for the door, hearing his smooth, velvety laughter on my way out.

I hadn't really been hungry when I made my bratty declaration, my stomach too jumbled with nerves and anxiety to even consider food, but instead of going back to the office, I pointed my car in the direction of Drip.

Just as I'd expected, Monica was behind the counter as I walked in, smiling at the customer across from her as she slid a small paper bag, containing something I knew from experience was delicious, across the counter.

"Hey," she greeted as I walked up. "How's it going?"

I placed my purse on the counter and with a weary sigh. "It would be better if I had a coffee the size of my face."

She gave me a scrutinizing look. "I can make that happen. Have a seat. I'm going on break in five and I'll join you."

That was perfect. I needed a friend at the moment if for no other reason than to help me get my head straight. I selected a table near the back, tucked into a corner for privacy, and waited. Sure enough, five minutes later, Monica sat down across from me, setting my boat-sized coffee on the table, along with two almond scones, one for her and one for me. "Those just came out of the oven," she noted, breaking off a piece of hers and popping it into her mouth.

The sugary smell hit me in the face, and suddenly the idea of food didn't seem so bad. Lifting the crumbly pastry, I bit off the edge and let out a delighted hum before washing it down with coffee.

"Thanks," I said around a second bite. "I needed that."

She raised her brows, her eyes dancing. "You want to tell me what has you all huffy today? You stormed in with this sour look on your face like someone had just stolen your parking spot and you were contemplating murder."

I took another drink to stall for a bit so I could build my courage. When that didn't work, I decided the best thing to do was just spit it out. I could trust her to keep it quiet. Gossip might have thrived in Whitecap, but friendship trumped the grapevine every day of the week. Unless I said otherwise, she'd keep this to herself.

"I had sex with Nate again. A *lot* of sex."

She proceeded to choke on the bite of scone she'd just taken. I waited patiently as she coughed and hacked before finally pulling in a full breath and wiping tears from her eyes. "You mean to tell me you went back for seconds? *You.* You?"

I nodded gravely. "And thirds. And fourths and fifths."

"Wow, that's just . . . Give me a second to wrap my head around this."

I waited again, nervously chewing on my thumbnail as the wheels in Monica's head spun.

Finally, after enough time to make me sweat, she asked, "How was it?"

I dropped my head on the table with a groan. I wasn't sure there was a word in the English language that could adequately describe how it was, but I had to give her something. "It was extraordinary," I confessed. "I mean, I remembered it being good the first time, but I'd almost convinced myself I'd built it up in my mind to be better than it actually was, you know?"

"Ah, yes. I've done that in the past. Not with Sam, but

with other exes. And when I went back for that ill-advised nostalgia bang, I'd been sorely disappointed."

"Exactly! Well, I didn't build Nate's skill up in my mind. If anything, my memory was downplayed because it was so damn good my brain could not compute."

She cocked her brows in question. "Then I don't get it. If it was so great, shouldn't you be in a good mood?"

"It's sexual frustration," I grumbled around the rim of my coffee cup. "Which shouldn't be happening yet since I had more sex than most humans can tolerate over the weekend. My tank is topped off and then some."

Monica nearly spit out the drink of tea she'd just taken. "Wow, babe. That's colorful."

"You know what I mean," I mumbled. "Anyway, he tried to kiss me in the office this morning, and when I put a stop to it, he got all pouty and grumpy."

"Wait." Monica held her hand up to stop me. "I don't understand. If the sex is as good as you claimed, why would you stop him?"

"Because we were at work," I insisted vehemently. "There have to be rules. This isn't a relationship, it's just sex. We can't just hook up at work whenever the hell we want or it'll start to complicate things."

She studied me intently. "What you mean to say is you could catch feelings."

"Yes! I mean, no! No, that's not—There are no feelings."

Her look said clear as day that she didn't believe me. Fortunately, she let it go. "Well, if you aren't worried about catching feelings, there's no problem. There's no real risk of complication, *and* it'll put you in a much better mood. Win-win."

She made it sound so damn easy, as if I were stressing out for no damn good reason. But . . . wait . . . *Was* I stressing out for no damn good reason? I could do this. I'd done it before. I knew how to separate sex from emotions. What the hell was I beating myself up for?"

I rose to my feet with determination. "You know what? You're right?"

"Usually am."

"I'm torturing myself for nothing. I'm going to take your suggestion. Damn, you're one smart cookie."

She laughed as I leaned down to place a kiss to her cheek. "Glad you finally realized that. Don't forget your coffee."

I skidded to a halt on my way to the door and whipped back around, snatching up my coffee cup and the rest of my scone. Then I hustled out of there as fast as my heels could take me.

My blood was churning by the time I got back to the office. Determination and hormones were raging like whitewater inside me. I crossed the threshold into Nate's office and slammed the door behind me.

He glanced up, the very picture of calm. "Feeling better?"

"I will be in about one minute," I said as I kicked off my heels and started in his direction. "Just as soon as you take off your pants."

Twenty-Four

NATE

Things between Luna and I were going better than I ever imagined. It had been two weeks since we started this . . . arrangement, and I still couldn't keep my hands off her. The moment she walked into a room, I was as hard as steel and raring to go.

She'd relented on her no-sex-in-the-office rule nearly as soon as she made it, and since then, we'd been tearing at each other's clothes every available opportunity we got. Now that Evan was no longer grounded and had even made some friends, a few of my evenings freed up. During those hours, I managed to sneak away to Luna's house, determined to make the most of every clandestine visit I could get. There'd yet to be another sleepover after that first one, but I was currently maneuvering pieces to make it happen as soon as fucking possible.

I couldn't get enough of her: her smell, her laugh, her smile, the clever things she'd say. The way she wrapped around me when I drove inside of her. I was quickly becoming addicted to everything about her, and it went against every instinct I had not to push for more.

It wasn't just about the sex. I wanted *her*, but I knew giving voice to those emotions was the fastest way to send her running. I wasn't a stupid man; she had one foot out the door at all times, just looking for a reason to pull the plug on us. But I also knew she was feeling the same things I was.

I saw it in the way she looked at me when she thought I couldn't see, in the brightness of the smile when she forgot to keep that guard up. I saw it in the way her eyes glistened every time I sank deep inside her, and felt it in the way she touched me, how she held on tight, like she was afraid I would drift through her fingers like smoke.

The past year had been so full of chaos, I hadn't seen Luna coming. She sneaked up on me like a goddamn ninja, burrowing her way under my skin and into my bones. I hadn't expected those kinds of feeling for anyone, but most especially her. She'd gone from being my enemy to the one thing I couldn't hold on to tight enough. I wanted all of her. I wanted to make her happy, and I knew, if she just gave me a chance, I could. But I had to tread carefully,

I was playing the long game. Patience was key, something I wasn't necessarily known for. But for her I would try.

Her moans turned to whimpers as her walls tighten around my driving cock. My balls drew up and I had to fight back the need to pour myself inside her. I wanted to make this last as long as possible. I wanted to feel every quiver and quake from her release.

"Oh, God. *Nate*. It's so good."

She had that right. It was bliss. Pure, unadulterated, agonizing bliss. From my vantage point standing over her, I could see my cock slide in and out, glistening with her arousal. The view alone was enough to send me over, but not before her. Never before her.

"Get there, moonbeam," I ordered, as I reached between her thighs to press my thumb against that bundle of nerves. She was already close, I could feel it in how tight she was squeezing me. That one touch was all it took to send her soaring over the edge. Her arms flew up over her head, her knuckles white from gripping the edge of my desk, and I rode her through it, pounding into her hot, wet sheath.

Her walls clenched around me like a vise as she called out my name, her pussy squeezing until I couldn't possibly hold back any longer. I exploded with a curse, stars bursting behind my eyelids as intense, almost painful, pleasure slammed into me. Every goddamn time. I never got used to how good it was.

"I'll never get used to this," she panted, mirroring my thoughts as her breath came in short bursts, like she just ran a marathon. "How good it always is. Every single time. It doesn't make sense; we should've worked each other out of our systems by now."

I forced my shaky limbs to cooperate, pulling out of her and holding out a hand to help her sit up. "Careful there, moonbeam. You're dangerously close to bruising my ego."

She let out a tired laugh, smacking me weakly in the belly with the back of her hand before hopping off my desk on wobbly legs and readjusting her skirt. "You know that's not what I meant." She smiled at me, and any animosity I'd been feeling washed away. Her skin was flushed with pleasure, her hair slightly mussed in the most perfect way. She was beautiful always, but like this . . . Christ, she took my breath away. "If anything, it was a compliment."

"Then I'll try to take it as such," I muttered at I tucked my spent dick back into my pants. "Come over tonight." The words spilled out before I could stop them, but I would have been lying if I said I regretted them.

She looked at me with bright eyes, the amber depths sparkling with curiosity. "To your apartment?"

"Last I checked, that was still where I lived."

"Much to Evan's dismay," she said with a throaty, sexy laugh. That was another thing I hadn't been expecting, just how close she and my daughter had become. For the past couple weeks, they'd been two peas in a pod. Evan would swing by the office almost every day after school before starting her shift at my parents' store, and the two of them would sit and giggle and snicker at God only knew what. Being the parent, and a male, I'd been told on multiple occasions that I wouldn't understand what it was they were talking about. Part of me worried, but the other part was grateful I didn't have to hear about it.

At some point, Evan had gone to Luna for makeup tips, because the next thing I knew, the raccoon eyeliner was gone, and my baby girl's natural beauty was put on display for everyone to see. I'd loved it at first, until she started coming home and telling me about the boys in her classes who had suddenly started talking to her.

She and Luna had even exchanged numbers and texted from time to time, and one weekend, I took Evan back over to Luna's, not so she could clean, but so Luna could teach her more about gardening. They'd spent the entire day at it without once coming up for air. I was pretty sure if I hadn't brought them something to eat, they would have skipped every meal.

I loved that my girl had a woman in her life she could

share those kinds of experiences with. Even before Amber proved herself to be the worst mother on the planet, she hadn't done those kinds of things with her daughter. She couldn't be bothered.

"I see you and my girl are still ganging up on me about that."

"There are a million beautiful rental properties around town," she said as she tucked her blouse back into her skirt. "Or hell, you could buy something." She waggled her brows before adding, "You know you can afford it."

Whether or not I could afford it wasn't the issue. It was the simple fact I hadn't found anything I liked enough to invest in. "I'll find something eventually. In the meantime, the apartment works." I circled back around to the original topic, refusing to let her off the hook. "So, tonight?"

Trepidation shone in her eyes as she asked, "Is Evan going over to a friend's house or something?"

And there it was. "No. She'll be home. I just figured, you could come over and we could all hang out. I'll cook a dinner that'll knock you on your ass, then maybe the three of us can watch a movie or something?"

She let out a heavy sigh. "Nate." I knew that tone, the hint of warning it held. And I fucking hated it. "You know we can't do that."

I wanted to throw my arms out and ask why the fuck

not, but before I got a chance, the sensor I'd installed on the front door so Luna and I wouldn't be caught with our pants down—literally—rang out, alerting me that we had a visitor.

"That'll be your two thirty, Ms. Hassleback," Luna said, snapping right back into assistant mode perfectly. "I'll be right outside if you need me."

"Luna," I said quietly before she could make her escape. "We're not done with this conversation."

She gave me a curt nod, her expression less than happy as she turned to walk out, and as she moved through the doorway, I could have sworn her knees were shaking.

She'd gotten lucky, either that or she'd packed my schedule so tight I barely had time to take a piss the rest of the day. Before I knew it, five o'clock had come and gone, and she'd snuck off like a goddamn coward so she could avoid the conversation. It pissed me off to no end, and I had to work hard to get that under control as I locked up the office by myself and headed to the general store to pick up my daughter.

Having spotted me through the windows, my mom scuttled out from behind the register as I pulled open the door and met me at the door.

"Everything okay?" I asked as I took in the harried expression her face. "What's the matter? Is it Evan?"

"No." She shook her head, looking flustered. "Well, I mean yes, but not how you think. Something happened not long after she got here." She held up her hand to silence me when I started to ask. "I don't know what, and I didn't ask because I didn't want to push, but something happened to change her disposition. She went from cheerful and on top of the world to sad and droopy. Poor girl's hardly said more than a handful of words in the past few hours. We gave her work to do in the back so she didn't have to deal with customers, and your dad's been keeping an eye on her."

My heart sank. Things had been so good for Evan the past couple weeks; I hated that something could have happened to change that. "I'll talk to her," I reassured my mom. "I'll figure out what's wrong and get her sorted out."

She wrung her hands in front of her and blew out a relieved sigh. "Okay, good. Because I don't want to see her go back to how it was. She's an amazing kid. She deserves to be happy."

I couldn't have agreed more, and I intended to make sure that was exactly what happened. "I'll take care of it," I promised. "In the meantime, how about you run back and get her while I pick up a few things I need to make dinner tonight?"

Mom reached up and cupped my check affectionately. "You're such a good dad. I'm proud of you, son."

That worked wonders to lessen the anger I'd been holding since leaving work. Now I had to get my daughter back to rights.

As I gathered ingredients for dinner, I wondered if there would ever come a time when I could go at least a day without *something* going wrong.

Twenty-Five

NATE

I kept glancing at Evan from the corner of my eye as I drove home. Sure enough, my mom had been right. Something had happened to kill that light that had finally started to shine again.

She hung her head as if trying to hide behind the curtain of her hair. Her shoulders were slumped like she was attempting to curl in on herself. I tried to start a conversation a couple times, but all I got were short answers with as few words as possible

When we got home, I asked if she wanted to help me with dinner, since she'd shown an interest in learning to cook from my mother, but she started right for the stairs, announcing she had homework.

I chopped and sautéed, boiled and strained. I threw myself into cooking, all the while, my head was spinning.

Things were unsteady with the two most important women in my life, and somehow, fucking *somehow*, I had to figure out how to fix it. Once dinner was ready, I called Evan, hoping that something might have shaken loose in the last hour, and she'd come downstairs like nothing had happened.

I wasn't so lucky. She skulked down the stairs and slunk into her chair. "What is this?"

Ah, she speaks, I thought, hoping for a breakthrough. "Shrimp and mussel linguine with a garlic butter sauce."

I'd done a pretty damn good job if I did say so myself, and the whole apartment smelled incredible, but as I started eating, all Evan did was push the food around on her plate with her fork.

"Everything okay?" I asked, silently willing her to tell me.

"It's fine," she muttered, keeping her head down.

I tried again. "How was your day?"

I didn't even get a verbal response that time, just a shrug. That did it.

"All right, that's it," I snapped, my tone much harsher than I intended, but for Christ's sake, how much was a man supposed to endure, huh? "Something's going on, and I want to know what it is right now, damn it."

There was a short sniffle, then Evan burst into tears.

"Ah, fuck. Fuck me," I grunted as I shot back in my

chair and moved to my daughter. Crouching down beside her, I wrapped her in my arms and held her tight as her tears soaked the shoulder of my shirt. "Jesus, sweetheart. I'm sorry. I didn't mean to snap at you like that. Please don't cry, honey."

I considered myself a pretty tough guy, or at least I liked to think I was. But when it came to female tears, I was more worthless than tits on a bull. But when they were my daughter's tears? It took me to my fucking knees.

"I'm sorry, Evan. I swear. Please, just stop crying, yeah? I won't yell again. If you don't want to tell me what's wrong, that's fine. I won't ask again."

She pulled back, reaching up to rub the wet from her face with the heels of her palms. "I-it's okay. It wasn't you. You didn't make me cry."

I reached back and grabbed the chair I'd abandoned, pulling it forward so I could sit down while still close enough to hug her if necessary. "You want to tell me what it's about then?"

"It was Mom," she confessed in a barely-there voice.

My back went stiff, but I tried my hardest to keep a neutral tone. "What happened?"

She let out a sound of disgust and shook her head. "It's so stupid, really. I shouldn't be upset. It's not like I didn't already know what she was going to say."

I stopped her before she could go off on a tangent and

get lost on the journey. "Ev, sweetheart. Tell me what happened."

She inhaled deeply and released it nice and slow before diving in. "Well, there's this dance coming up at school next month." Ah Christ, if this involved a boy, I was going to be sick. "Apparently there's some town tradition that all the girls in my grade and their moms are supposed to put everything together for the dance. It's a pretty big deal, I guess."

"Shit, I remember that dance. They still do that?"

"I guess so," she said with a shrug. "Anyway, they were talking about it in homeroom today, making this big deal out of it, and I thought it sounded kind of cool."

Oh shit.

"I figured I'd call Mom and tell her about it. There's still a lot of time between now and the dance, and I thought maybe, if she had enough notice, she could come up here on a weekend or something and do it with me. I know it's a long drive, but road trips are kind of fun."

A ball of lead had formed right in the pit of my stomach. "That was a good idea, honey. What did she say?"

"She said—" The sniffles started again and the tears that had just begun to dry up grew in intensity. "She said she couldn't because she met some guy. She's been seeing him for a while now, and he just accepted a job in San Antonio. She's moving there with him."

The hardest thing I'd ever done in my life was keep my mouth shut and not talk shit about my daughter's mother to or around her. Just when I thought I couldn't possibly hate the woman more, the woman I'd once pledge to love until death parted us, she did something to prove there was a whole new level of hate I hadn't even reached yet.

"Honey, I—" I didn't know what to say, how to make it better, how to make up for the fact that her mother was a raging, despicable bitch. I wish I could have told her she was better off, but I couldn't talk about her mom that way without hurting her, no matter how true it was. "I wish I knew what to say to stop the pain. If I could, I'd take it all away."

Those big blue eyes, the ones I'd fallen head over heels for twelve years ago, lifted to meet mine. "She's doing this because she's mad at me. She wanted me to choose her over you. She wanted to win. But I didn't do that, so she's mad."

Feeling my nails digging into my palms, leaving crescent shapes indents in my skin, I worked to unclench my fists. "Did she actually say that to you?"

She shook her head. "No. Not right out. But I know her. That sad thing is, it almost worked. I let her get to me, I let her scare me. That's why I was such a brat for so long." Her bottom lip trembled, nearly doing me in. "Daddy, I'm really sorry."

She collapsed against me. "Oh, hey. Hey now." I held on tight, running my hand over her silky blonde hair. "You don't have anything to apologize for." It felt like someone had shoved their fist into my chest and squeezed my heart. Anticipation lashed at my skin. This felt big, like the breaking point I'd desperately been trying to get us to for the better part of a year. "Can you tell me what you were scared of?"

"Th-that you'll stop l-loving me the way you stopped loving h-her," she confessed on a broken sob. "I know I'm not your real daughter, not by blood, or whatever, and I was scared that you'd decide to give me up too."

Everything inside of me broke in that very moment. Nothing worked the way it was supposed to. My heart shattered, my lungs couldn't pull in enough air. It would have hurt less if I'd lain down in the middle of traffic and let a goddamn semi run over me.

"Evan." My voice was jagged, like I'd just gargled with gravel. "Honey, is that what you really think?"

She pulled the sleeves of her hoodie over her hands, curling her fists tight and wiping at more tears. "Not anymore. But I did for a little while because I let Mom get in my head. After the divorce went through, she said we weren't a family anymore, and you'd probably meet another woman you'd want to have your own kids with and I should expect you wouldn't have time for me anymore."

I'd never felt such white hot, intense rage in all my life, rage that could consume me until I was nothing but a vibrating ball of fury, in danger of destroying everything in my path. My skin was crawling.

"That is *never* going to happen. Do you understand me?" At the deep, angry rumble in my voice, her head shot up, her wide eyes jerking to me. "Whether or not I meet another woman and have more kids, you will always be my daughter, and I will *always* have time for you. Nothing will ever change that."

"But—"

"No buts," I interrupted. "I can't begin to understand why your mom thought it was okay to say something like that to you, but whatever is eating at her bad enough to make her to say something so cruel to her own child is her problem to deal with, not yours, and not mine. You are *my* daughter, Evan; you have been from the moment I first laid eyes on you. The first time you lifted your chubby little arms because you wanted me to pick you up, I was a goner. It's the closest to love at first sight I've ever come, sweetheart. No one and nothing will ever change that. You're my kid, and that will remain true until the earth stops spinning."

She smiled. It was small and trembled with emotion,

but it was the most beautiful thing I'd ever seen in all my life. "I love you too," she said softly. "Just in case you weren't sure because I've been acting like such a jerk for so long."

"I know, honey," I said, pulling her in for another hug, needing desperately to hold her and remind myself she was mine, she was here with me, healthy, and on her way to happy. "I never doubted that. Even when you were acting like a little jerk. And screw tradition. If you want, I'll team up with you to work on that dance. You just say the word and I'll make it happen. I'm a lawyer, so if anyone tries to fight me, I'll grind them to dust."

She let out a little giggle that worked wonders in loosening the knot that had been twisting in my chest. "I was thinking I'd ask Luna. But thanks."

"Any time."

There were a few beats of silence before she spoke again. "Um, Dad?"

"Yeah, kiddo?"

"Do you think you could maybe let me go? I'm pretty hungry, and the food smells really good."

I stood on the balcony, a cigar in one hand, a glass of scotch in the other. By the time Evan had gone to bed, she'd been my bright, happy girl once again. Unfortunately, I hadn't been able to let go quite so easily.

I still held that anger, that white-hot rage, churning in my gut as I stared at the ebony ocean in the distance. There was only one person I wanted to talk to, one person I wanted to vent everything I felt so I didn't have that goddamn two-ton weight sitting on my chest.

I didn't let myself overthink it as I set my glass down and picked up my cellphone, scrolled to her number, and hit the green button.

It rang three times, and I started to think maybe she was asleep and wouldn't answer, when the call suddenly connected and Luna's velvety voice came through the line. "Nate?"

Just that was enough to relieve some of that weight. "Hey." My own voice came out gruff and low. "Did I wake you?"

"No, I was just lying in bed, reading. Is everything okay? You sound different than normal."

"Not really, no." I puffed on the cigar in my hand for a moment before snuffing it out in the ashtray and reaching for my glass.

"Are you smoking a cigar right now?"

"And drinking scotch." I gave the glass a little shake so she could hear the rattle of the ice cubes. "It's been a shitty night and I needed to unwind a bit."

There wasn't the slightest hesitation as she asked, "What's wrong?"

"Evan finally opened up and told me what's been bothering her this whole time," I replied flatly.

There was a short pause across the line. "Really? But isn't that a good thing? That she finally opened up to you?"

"Yeah, it is. We worked out a lot of shit, and I hope the two of us really turned a corner. But some of the things she told me . . ." I closed my eyes and inhaled deeply, trying to keep my cool. "I can't shake this rage, Luna. It's eating at me."

I heard her breathing through the phone. "Then talk to me," she said softly, gently. "Talk to me and get it out so it can't do any more damage."

That right there was why I called her, why I needed her. Hell, why I was already half in love with her, if not more.

I did as she'd ordered, giving her all of it, pouring out the poison until nothing was left. I told her everything Evan had confessed to me from start to finish, and by the time I finished purging, I felt like myself again.

Silence stretched through the line for several moments once I finished, to the point I worried the call had dropped. But then she spoke. "Okay, first off, I've never met your ex, but I hate her. I mean, *hate* her. San Antonio isn't far enough away. I want to hunt her down and rip all her hair out, and I mean all of it, Nate. I want to use tweezers and pluck her nose hairs one at a time."

I couldn't help but laugh.

"She doesn't know this, and being her father, you can't actually come right out and say it, but she's better off without that woman in her life." My mind went back to the conversation I'd listened in on, and my gut was telling me Luna was speaking from experience.

"I had the exact same thought. I had to swallow the words down."

"Second, that whole dance tradition needed to be done away with like ten years ago. Times have changed. Families come in all different shapes and sizes, and not all of them include the standard mother and father pairing. Someone needs to talk to the school board and stop that tradition, or at least change it to be inclusive of all the different family dynamics out there."

I smiled so big my cheeks ached. God, I was gone for this woman. "Well, I'm glad you feel so passionately about that, because Evan mentioned asking you if you wanted to team up with her."

"Hell yeah, I would," she answered without a single blink, without a thought. Just like that. My girl wanted something, and Luna jumped at the chance to give it to her.

Moving away from the railing, I sat in one of the cheap plastic chairs since our old patio furniture wouldn't fit. "You're fucking incredible, you know that?" I asked in a low, raspy voice.

"Of course I do. It was you who was slow on the uptake."

My chuckle shook loose the rest of that knot, taking the last remaining bits of anger with it. "Kicking myself for taking so long to realize it. Thanks for the talk."

I could hear the smile in her voice as she said, "Anytime, Nate. Goodnight."

"Goodnight, baby."

I pulled the phone away from my ear and disconnected as the words *I love you* filtered through my brain.

Twenty-Six

LUNA

THIS WAS the very definition of heaven, at least as far as I was concerned. I stretched my overused limbs before curling deeper into Nate's side. This was quickly becoming one of my favorite places to be, right here, wrapped in his arms, after sex.

There hadn't been many instances for this kind of snuggling lately, but when Evan had swung by the office earlier to tell Nate she'd been invited to a sleepover at a friend's house, a sense of giddiness tore through me before he'd had a chance to answer. He asked her question after question, everything to ensure his daughter's safety, before casting his eyes to me and smiling in a way that warmed me from the inside out. I hadn't been able to stop myself from returning it.

He said yes, after laying down some ground rules, of course, and when she went skipping out of the building, he'd given me a look that could have melted the iceberg that downed the Titanic as he braced his hands on my desk and leaned in to speak against my lips. "I hope you aren't planning on sleeping tonight, because I'm staying over."

My lady parts had practically stood up and danced a jig. Now we were both sated, worn out, and snuggled together in my super-soft sheets.

I hummed contently as he softly traced random patterns on my hip with the tips of his fingers. "I know this is only our second one, but I'm starting to really like these sleepovers."

"Me too," he said on a chuckle. He trailed his fingers along my side, over my ribs and the side of my breast. "You know," he started softly, "we could have more of these if you weren't so determined to keep us a secret."

I let out a small laugh. "You're funny," I said in a teasing tone. "You know we can't do that."

He tucked his chin into his neck so he could look down at me. "Why not" he asked, genuine curiosity swimming in his gaze.

I pulled back to get a better look at his face. "Wait. You're serious?"

"Well, yeah. I mean, think about it. What we have is

pretty great. What's so wrong with people finding out? Would it really be the end of the world?"

"I think you might've forgotten how small towns operate," I teased, trying to bring levity back into a conversation that had suddenly gotten way too serious. "Letting people know we're sleeping together is asking for trouble. We'll be bombarded with questions, curious stares, people speculating on when or if you're going to propose."

He lifted his brows until they nearly kissed his hairline. "So?"

I stayed silent, waiting to see if he was messing with me. When it became obvious he wasn't, I sat up and pulled the sheet around my chest to cover my nakedness. "Okay, if that's not enough, how about the fact your daughter would find out? Or your parents? I don't know about you, but that seems like a lot of trouble to go through for a hookup."

He pushed himself up, resting his back against the headboard, his face hard as stone and his eyes flashing with a brewing storm. "This isn't just a hookup," he said in the voice akin to a growl. "You know that, so don't act like what I'm saying is news to you."

My heart began to beat staccato against my ribs, the saliva in my mouth drying up like I'd sucked on a cotton ball. "Nate." I blinked wide eyes. "You know what this is, we talked about this. You knew the score from the very beginning."

"That's true, but the score changed," he said definitively. "Tell me you don't feel for me what I feel for you. Tell me you don't want to be with me, and really truly mean it, and I'll agree that's all we are. But you have to mean it. No lies."

"What are you doing?" I asked my voice rising as panic stirred in my blood. "You can't just change the rules."

"Fuck the rules!" he barked so fiercely I jumped. "Fuck the rules and fuck what people think. What we have is fucking incredible. You know that. This thing between us, it doesn't come around every day. Hell, most people are lucky to feel it just once. I love you."

"Stop," I croaked as the air whooshed out of my lungs.

"No, I won't stop. I love you, and you love me, damn it. This right here, this is what's real." He took my hand and placed it against his chest, right over the steady beat of his heart. "I know that because the only time I've ever felt this, ever known something down to my soul, was the first time I saw Evan."

"Don't say that," I pleaded. "Nate, just stop. Don't ruin this."

He went from angry to passionate to gentle so fast my head began to spin. "I'm not trying to ruin it, baby." He took my face in his hands, his touch so tender it nearly brought tears to my eyes. "I'm trying to make you see how right this is. I can make you happy, Luna. I swear to God. I can make you happier than you've ever been if you'll let me."

I jerked my face from his hold and rolled off the mattress before he had a chance to grab me. Snatching the nightgown he'd stripped off me earlier, I yanked it back on in short, jerky movements. "I'm happy with things exactly how they've been," I snapped angrily.

"Well I'm not." He climbed out of the bed and pulled on his discarded jeans. The king-sized mattress between us might as well have been the Grand Canyon with how far from him I suddenly felt. With three words, he'd stuck a knife right into my heart. "I want more. I want everything. But more than that, I want to give you the same. And, damn it, I want my girl to have you too. She deserves you, Luna. We both do. And you deserve us. How do you not see that?"

"I told you from the very beginning I don't do relationships."

He shot back to angry. "Well, I hate to break it to you, honey, but that's what you've been doing with me this whole goddamn time!"

"It isn't!"

"Jesus Christ," he snapped, reaching up to rake his

fingers through his hair. "I feel like I'm arguing with a goddamn kid."

I crossed my arms over my chest, an irrational wave of anger slamming into me and threatening to wash me away. Things had been so good between us. Who the hell did he think he was, coming in here and asking for more, ruining something so freaking perfect? "Then maybe you should leave," I clipped.

He rocked back on one foot, his features blanking from one moment to the next. "Is that really what you want? For me to leave right now?"

I opened my mouth to say yes, but couldn't force the lie out. "Gah!" I cried, grabbing my hair in frustration. "This is ridiculous! I don't know why we're fighting right now."

He moved so fast I didn't have time to brace. One moment he was standing on the opposite side of the bed and the next he was taking my face in his hands again and leaning down to rest his forehead against mine. "I know this is scary," he said gently. "But all you have to do is trust me, moonbeam. Just trust me. You do that, you take the leap with me, and I swear to God, I'll catch you."

How did he not realize how terrifying what he was asking me to do was? Trusting anyone like that was impossible. The closest I'd ever come was Cheyanne and Monica. I had nothing more to give than that.

"I know you didn't have the greatest example of what it looked like to be in love or in a healthy relationship, but I can show you."

His words penetrated the fog clouding my brain. Time seemed to slow as I grabbed hold of his wrists and pulled his hands away before taking a big, careful step back. "What did you just say?"

Confusion marred his brow, deepening those indentions between his eyes. "What?"

"About not having the greatest example." Cold washed over my whole body. "What would make you say that?"

"I—" He stopped and pulled in a long, steady breath. "I overheard the call you had with your mom a while back."

"You—" The blood began to rush in my ears so fast I barely heard anything else. It was like a swarm of bees had been let loose in my skull, a constant, nagging sound that drowned everything else out. "You eavesdropped on my phone call?"

"I was worried about you," he declared. "One minute you were fine, then your phone rang and all the color drained out of your face. I had to make sure you were all right, so I listened in."

"You had no right!" I boomed, that slow simmer of anger that had been building inside of me finally boiling over. "That was a private conversation and you had no goddamn right listening in like that!"

"Goddamn it, Luna. Stop and look at what you're doing right now. You aren't mad I listened in on your call. You're scared. You're fucking terrified, and you're picking a fight so you don't have to feel that, because you think it would be better to be mad than scared."

"Don't act like you know me," I hissed as goosebumps erupted over my skin, because the truth was, he was right. I was scared out of my fucking mind, and I couldn't handle it.

His shoulders slumped in defeat. "But I do know you, Luna. Probably better than anyone. And you can't stand that, because it means I got past those walls."

His eyes felt like they were burrowing down into my soul as he stared at me. When I didn't say anything, because all the words had dried up in my mouth, his whole body slumped. He shook his head and the look on his face flayed me open. Like I'd just ripped his heart to pieces.

"I can't go back to how we were," he said quietly. "Even if I could, I wouldn't do it, because it's not enough. I want all of you."

My vision blurred as tears welled in my eyes, spilling down onto my cheeks. "What if I can't do that?" I whispered. "What if what we have right now is all I can give you?"

"I want it all, Luna. I can't settle. I just can't."

I watched in silence, feeling like my heart was being squeezed in a vise as he got dressed. He stopped on his way to the door, taking my chin in his hand and tilting my face up so he could place the softest, most agonizing kiss to my lips. Then he gutted me with his words.

"I'm in love with you. I wish you were brave enough to say the same."

Twenty-Seven

LUNA

NATE and I had been broken up for a week.

No. That wasn't right. In order to break up, two people had to consent to forming a relationship, that they were a couple in a way they both agreed on. That hadn't been the case for Nate and me. We weren't broken up since we had never been a couple. Because I'd been too stubborn and scared and cowardly to accept the truth, what was already very real, and agree that we were more than a no-strings, casual hookup.

He'd told me he loved me. He told me he wanted to make me happy, that he knew what we had was the real deal. He'd asked me to trust him, to take that leap and trust he'd be there to catch me. And I ruined it. The happiest I'd ever been, and I fucking *ruined* it.

The look on his face when I'd asked him why we

couldn't just keep things simple haunted me. I saw it every time I closed my eyes. Heartbreak and disappointment. I couldn't think of a worse combination. I'd never had my heart broken before because I'd never let anyone in enough to have that kind of power. Until Nate.

I'd ruined us because I was so scared of getting my heart broken that I wasn't smart enough to realize it had already happened, and that I'd done it to myself. How was that for irony?

It had been a week since Nate told me it was all or nothing before walking away, and I wasn't sure there'd ever been a time in my life when I'd been more miserable. I thought working with him would be awkward once things between us ran their course, but that didn't begin to cover it. Seeing him day after day, wanting him, missing him like I'd lost a part of me, only to be met head-on with chilly indifference was absolute torture.

He never met my eyes for more than two seconds, had taken to sending his requests to me through email when I was only a wall away, and otherwise pretended I didn't exist unless there was no choice, in which case he was so polished and professional, you'd have thought he was a fucking robot.

Each morning I woke up to the sun shining through my bedroom curtains was another day of misery. I couldn't stand the stunning, happy view outside my bedroom windows so I'd begun keeping the blinds drawn at all times. That bright, cheery sun and those playful lapping waves felt like a slap in the face. What right did the sun have to shine when I felt like warmed-over shit?

By Friday, I was so broken I decided to use one of those vacation days I'd bargained for. I sent Nate an email telling him I would be out of the office for the day, then shut everything down, crawled back into bed, and pulled the covers over my head. I stayed like that for most of the day, only coming out of my little cocoon to use the bathroom or when the need for food grew too strong.

For the next couple days, I lived in that bed, eating boxes of crackers and cookies, entire bags of chips or pints of ice cream beneath my cozy blanket fortress and watching Hallmark movies simply because the love stories made me cry and I deserved it.

Sure, they weren't as good as my audio books, but I refused to allow myself that luxury. I derived pleasure from those romance novels, and I didn't deserve anything that made me feel good at the moment.

By the time Sunday rolled around, I started to think my life would be a hell of a lot simpler if I just stayed in that bed forever. That was how my friends found me on a bright, lovely, blasphemous Sunday afternoon.

"Oh, God," I heard from the doorway of my bedroom. I might have moved, or at least turned my head, but I recognized the voice and knew it was only a matter of seconds before she came in. And of course she'd let herself in with the key I gave her for emergencies. "What's that smell?"

"It smells like B.O. and chocolate."

A third voice declared, "Are we sure she's not dead in there? I really don't want to pull the covers back and find a dead body. I don't have the stomach for that sort of thing."

I flipped the covers down and twisted my head to see Cheyanne, Georgia, Monica, and Evan standing in my bedroom doorway.

"Oh. Hello," I said in a voice devoid of all emotion.

"Oh, thank God." Monica let out a breath and placed a hand over her heart. "She's alive."

"She doesn't look it." Evan's top lip curled up as she covered her nose with the collar of her shirt. "Doesn't smell like it either."

Cheyanne started toward me, the smile on her face one you might expect to see on a person trying to talk someone off the ledge . . . literally. "Hi," she said in a soft, cheery voice. "Hey, it's good to see you. How about we get you out of bed, huh?"

"I live here now," I informed her, patting the Egyptian cotton sheet that was now covered in chip crumbs and melted chocolate.

"Yeah, I can see that. But it might be a good idea to get you in the shower and these sheets in the washer."

"Those sheets are toast," Monica noted. "Best to just take them out back and burn them."

I ignored her heartless suggestion and answered Cheyanne. "Oh, no thank you. I'm just fine here. You don't happen to have a pizza with you, do you? I ordered one a while ago and haven't heard the doorbell. It usually doesn't take this long. Then again, I'm not sure when I ordered it. I've stopped looking at the clock. Did you come across the delivery guy?"

"Nope, no delivery guy, sunshine." Monica came at me, her demeanor a lot less soothing than Cheyanne's. "Now, up you go." She grabbed hold of the covers and threw them off the bed.

I let out a pained groan.

"You're going to bathe that stink off you while we fumigate this room. Then we're going to talk."

Snatching one of my pillows, I held it over my face to block everything out and declared, "I don't wanna!"

"Too damn bad."

I let out a yelp as she grabbed me by the ankle and dragged me off the bed. With no other choice, I threw my hands up and relented, "Okay, fine. I'll get in the shower."

Georgia offered me a kind smile. "Great. We'll be downstairs when you're finished."

To which, Monica added, "Do *not* get back in that bed," as she jabbed her finger at the food-stained sheets.

It took two washes to get my hair clean, and I'd had to scour my teeth with my electric toothbrush until they felt smooth, but by the time I stepped out of the bathroom, I felt a little more human. I just wasn't sure that was necessarily a good thing.

I followed the scent of freshly brewed coffee to my kitchen where almost everyone I loved sat gathered around my island.

"This feels like an intervention," I muttered as I moved to the coffee maker and poured myself a cup.

"Luna?"

At Evan's soft, uncertain tone, I turned around and joined the little group at the island, standing directly across from the beautiful girl with the worried blue eyes. "Yeah, honey?"

She chewed on her bottom lip, a nervous habit I'd noticed, and asked, "Are you okay?"

I wasn't, not even close, but I also wasn't going to dump my problems on her. After all, I had no one but myself to blame. "Yeah," I said with a strained smile. "I'm okay. Just a little sad."

"Are you sad because you and my dad broke up?"

My eyes went wide and shot over to Monica. "Are you kidding me? You *told*?"

"Don't look at me," she cried defensively. "I didn't say a word!"

"Wait, you told her and not me?" Cheyanne pointed a finger in Monica's direction while looking at me, then whipped around on Monica. "She told you and you didn't tell me?"

"All right," Georgia started in a firm, no-nonsense tone. "That's quite enough of that. You ladies are about to do my head in." She heaved out a sigh and shook her head. "Cheyanne, get over it. You know how it goes with secrets between friends. You keep them no matter what. Luna, you stop your blaming. No one told anyone anything. You and my boy aren't nearly as good at hiding things as you think you are."

I flushed and lowered my head to hide my embarrassment.

"Grandma's right. You two were always smiling at each other, and you've both been in way better moods. Plus, every time I came by the office, either he was sitting on your desk really close or you were sitting on his really close. Either way, it was gross. No fourteen-year-old girl should see her dad mooning over a woman, no matter how much I like you."

Monica laughed outright while Cheyanne at least had the decency to try and hide it behind her hand.

"So is that why you're sad? Because you broke up? Because Dad's been in the worst mood all week long."

"Really?" I wasn't sure it was healthy that I got a little thrill at that news, but I did. He'd just been so cool all week that he wasn't giving a damn thing away.

"Yeah. He's been moping around the apartment and staring into space. And he's snapping at every little thing. He got onto me yesterday for breathing too loud." She leaned in, her face a mask of seriousness as she repeated, "*Breathing*. I can't control that! Who can control that?"

"All right, sweetie." Georgia gave her granddaughter's hand a pat to calm her down. "We all understand."

Evan pulled in a couple of deep breaths, and when she'd calmed down, she started again. "What happened?" she asked, her face awash with sadness and concern. "Did he do something? I'm sure if you tell him what he did, he'll fix it. He's a really great guy. I don't understand why you don't like him anymore."

Oh God, this girl was killing me. I blinked furiously to keep the tears at bay. "Oh, honey, it's not that."

"Then what?" she demanded to know. "I know I'm just a kid, but I'm not stupid. I know you made my dad really happy. Like, happier than he *ever* was with my mom. He deserves that. And I know he made you happy too, because if he didn't you wouldn't have been moping around in your bed for days, stinking the place up."

I had to curl my lips between my teeth to keep from laughing, because from the fierce determination on her face, she wasn't joking, and the last thing I wanted to do was insult her.

"He didn't do anything, Evan. In fact, he was perfect. It was me. I'm the one who messed it all up. Some people aren't built for relationships. I really, *really* liked your dad, but I've just got too much baggage."

"You mean your mom?"

"Oh babe," Cheyanne whispered with gentle sympathy. She was the only one who knew the full story of my mother. Aside from the small bit I'd given to Evan, I'd never said anything about her. She was my shameful secret I hadn't wanted getting out.

"That's a large part of it, yes."

Something changed in Evan just then. Her expression grew firm and her body language changed. Hell, even the atmosphere shifted around us. "So because you have a screwed-up mom and I have a screwed-up mom, does that mean I'm not going to be built for relationships either?"

"What? No! Of course not! Evan, sweetie—"

"Because, by your way of thinking, that's exactly what it means. Because my mom didn't love me the way she was supposed to, I'll close myself off from relationships. I mean, isn't that exactly what you're doing right now?"

"I—" My mouth gaped open in complete shock. I'd just been played, and stupendously, by a freaking teenager. I narrowed my eyes and pointed at her accusingly. "Oh, you had that one planned down to the letter, didn't you?"

She blushed but didn't bother to hide her smile. "I had some help from Grandma."

I turned my scowl on an unrepentant Georgia as she threw her arm around her granddaughter's shoulders.

"Word around town all damn week was how miserable the two of you looked every time someone saw you. I don't know about you, but that seems pretty telling to me, and what it's telling me is the two of you are sprung for each other. Now, I'm going to give you my two cents, and that'll be the end of it. You can do with it what you want."

I braced, waiting for Georgia's words of wisdom.

"Whether or not you and my boy work out, you won't be any worse off than you are at this very moment. Love isn't a guarantee; it takes work. You have to fight for it. The only thing you're doing by refusing your heart what it wants is losing out on a chance to be happy, and if you ask me, that seems like a waste."

"You're not going to find many men better than my dad," Evan tacked on. "There are a ton of worse out there, but not many better."

"I know," I said on a whisper.

Monica came around the counter and took my face in her hands. "I told you, girl. When you finally found the man for you, it was going to knock you on your ass. And I'd be right there to say 'I told you so.'"

I let out a watery laugh. "I remember."

"Well." She leaned in close. "I told you so. Now what are you going to do about it?"

Twenty-Eight

LUNA

WHEN I WOKE up the following morning, I didn't bother putting on makeup or styling my hair. It would have been a lie, a mask to conceal the pain I'd been feeling the past several days. I didn't want to hide it. I wanted him to see, because it was the only way I could make sure he'd believe what I had to say.

I ditched the sweats I'd been living in for days and opted for a pair of black cigarette pants and a white button-down, but there was no jewelry, no embellishments. This was bare-bones Luna.

The thought of what I was about to do scared the living hell out of me, but I didn't have a choice. My friends were right. Evan was right. Georgia was right. I couldn't possibly feel any worse than I had over the past week, and I couldn't keep living that way. I needed to be brave. I couldn't shield myself from pain, not if it meant giving up something that meant everything to me.

By the time I pulled up in front of the office, my knees were shaking so badly I worried I'd fall face first onto the walkway and make a fool of myself. It was only by sheer determination that I managed to make it inside in one piece.

I couldn't remember a time in my life when I'd been so nervous. My heart was beating so hard I thought Nate might actually be able to hear it.

Moving past the waiting room, I dropped my purse onto my desk and headed straight for the break area at the back. With shaking hands, I fixed Nate's morning cup of coffee just how he liked it.

My whole body trembled so badly I was afraid I'd spill the coffee down the front of my shirt, but somehow, I made it through the open door of the office unscathed. I didn't bother knocking, I simply stepped inside and moved toward his desk, my eyes pinned to him the whole way. He didn't look up, but I knew he felt me the moment I walked in by the way his spine went rigid and his shoulder stiffened.

I closed the distance between us, the fragrance of leather and cloves, that sweet hint of tobacco, invading my senses as I set the coffee cup on his desk. I took a single step back clasping my hands in front of me to hide how nervous I was.

"I didn't know my father," I started, figuring it best to go back to the very beginning. "He left before I was old enough to realize I was supposed to miss him. I don't know why, I don't know who he was or where he went, but I've never missed him. I never felt like I was missing out on anything by not having a dad. My mom, on the other hand, didn't handle it so gracefully." I shook my head and smiled brittlely. "She's one of those women who's incapable of being single. She needs to be taken care of her; the problem is, the men she picks usually aren't up for the task. My mom has a very distinct type. If you're a loser, a worthless waste of air, or a blight on humanity, you're her type. But that doesn't stop her from pouring everything she is, everything she has, into those lousy relationships. She gives them everything, so there was never anything left over for me.

"When I was fourteen, her boyfriend at the time came into my room while I was sleeping." The air around me went electric, fire danced in Nate's eyes. But he didn't move, he didn't say a word. He simply waited for me to finish.

"He didn't do anything. He didn't get the chance. I

woke up as soon as he sat on the edge of my bed. He reached out and pulled the covers down. He talked about how beautiful I was. He said I had a young woman's body, and it made him feel things.

"I knew if I didn't get out of there something bad was going to happen, so I jumped up and ran as fast as I could. I ran to my mom's room. I told her what happened, what he did, what he said, how he made me feel." A bitter, manic laugh bubbled up in my throat. "And do you know what she said? She said if I hadn't been flaunting myself in front of him, he wouldn't have done what he did, that I'd been *asking* for it. She blamed me, a child no older than Evan, for a grown man behaving in such an obscene way. She accused me of being jealous of her, of wanting her man, her life. I made myself a promise right then and there that I would never, *ever* be like her.

"That wasn't the first piece of shit she brought around, and it was far from the last. I was more vigilant after that. I kept my bedroom door locked, kept a chair propped under the knob. I never felt unsafe again after doing that, but everything changed that night. I finally saw my mother for what she really was. I realized I would never be enough for her, and I would always come last to the men in her life, no matter how terrible they were.

"I had a pretty sizable nest egg before my company went under. I'd saved up enough that, if the worst happened, I'd be able to get by for a while until I got my feet back under me. But every time one of her boyfriends dumped her, my mother would come calling, and like an idiot, I would bail her out. Over and over again, like I was a fucking glutton for punishment or something. I wanted so badly for her to love me; I gave her what she asked for, thinking maybe she'd stick around that time. But she never did."

Nate spoke then, his voice low and raspy. "Then the worst happened, and when you needed her she wasn't there."

I didn't realize I'd started crying until one of the tears dripped off my chin and onto my hands. I let out a watery laugh and batted at my cheeks. "Yep. Pretty much. The last chunk of money I'd given her was a loan for cosmetology school so she could learn a trade and maybe start taking care of herself. Turns out, she gave it to her boyfriend and his buddy. Guess whatever they had going on was more important than trying to better herself.

"That's the guy you mentioned on that call?"

"Yep," I said bitterly. "The love of her life. Guess why she called me that day?"

Nate stood then, rounding his desk and resting his hips back against the edge as he crossed his arms over his broad chest. "I don't have to guess. After that story you just told me, it's pretty obvious."

"As sad as it is, my mom and Evan's would be tied in a competition for world's shittiest parent."

"I'm sorry, Luna."

"It's okay." I shook my head and pulled in a fortifying breath. "I mean it's not, not really. But I didn't tell you all of that because I want you to feel sorry for me."

Those stormy sea eyes burned into me. "Then why did you tell me?"

"Because I want you to understand why I am the way I am, why I was determined to never have a relationship or make a commitment."

His brows went up and I knew the moment he caught on to what I'd just said.

"*Was?*" he asked, stressing that one word.

"Well, I couldn't very well speak in the present tense. Not when I've gone and fallen in love with you."

His nostrils flared. He reached down to grip the edge of his desk, his knuckles turning white like he was fighting back the desire to reach out and grab me. "Say it again," he grunted.

The words came much easier the second time, and I had hope that maybe one day I could say them as easily as he did. "I'm in love with you. I want to give you all of me. I know I'll screw up from time to time, so you're going to need to bear with me, but I want to give you everything."

His arm lashed out faster than a snake striking. I yelped

as he grabbed me around the waist and yanked me to him, plastering my front to his and kissing me. His kiss was so full of emotion, the backs of my eyes began to burn.

When he finally pulled back, resting his forehead against mine, we both chugged air like we'd run a marathon at a dead sprint. "We're really doing this?"

"We are," I assured him, my heart swelling so damn big it was a wonder there was any room left in my chest. I bit down on my bottom lip as I summoned up the courage to say what came next. "And I might have found a solution to your whole apartment problem."

Nate smiled against my lips, and I could have sworn I tasted it. It tasted like sunshine on a hot summer day, like sugar and chocolate and everything good. "You have, have you?"

"Mm-hmm. You see, my house is awfully big for only one person. Plus, it would make life so much easier when it came to teaching Evan to garden."

"All good points."

"Then of course, there's the view from our bedroom."

He squeezed me tight and rained kisses across my face. "Sold," he declared triumphantly. "We'll move in this weekend."

My eyes went wide. "What about your lease?"

He harrumphed and waved that off like it was nothing.

"Please. I'm a lawyer, moonbeam. I can talk my way out of it."

"Then I guess you guys are moving in this weekend."

"Guess we are," he said softly, dragging the tip of his nose along the side of mine. "And Luna?"

"Hmm?"

"I meant what I said. I'm going to make you happier than you've ever been."

Oh, I had no doubt about that.

Epilogue

NATE

A MONTH and a half later

"I can't believe I let you talk me into this," I grumbled miserably. This was my personal hell. Everything from the strobe lights to the god-awful music to the sound of shrieking teenage girls was a nightmare. I'd gotten a headache the moment I walked into the high school gym, and it was getting worse with each passing minute.

True to her word, Luna had jumped at the opportunity to help Evan with the school dance. However, she'd also taken her complaints on the outdated tradition to the school board. After an impassioned speech that rallied several of the parents to her side, the tradition had officially been changed to include any guardian of a high school freshman who wanted to be involved.

There had been so many volunteers this year that the dance was being touted as the most successful in the school's history. I didn't care one way or the other about that. I just loved that my two girls found yet another common interest to bond over.

To say things had been great the past month and a half would have been an understatement. Under Luna's love and praise, my baby girl blossomed. Evan was the happiest I'd ever seen her. She had a whole crew of friends now, was making straight A's in school, and even though she'd finished paying off the damage she'd done to Luna's car all those months ago, she stayed on at Warren's General Store for no reason other than she loved the quality time she got to spend with her grandparents.

Just as Luna had suspected, Sunday dinners at the Warren house now included an inquisition on when I planned to propose to Luna and make an honest woman out of her, but I couldn't bring myself to care. And Luna didn't seem to mind either, which was good, considering the ring I'd bought for her had been burning a hole in my pocket for a while now. Evan already knew, having gone with me to pick it out, and was so excited she could barely see straight. I was just waiting for the right moment. I didn't have a clue when that would be, but I trusted I'd know when it presented itself.

"Oh, stop complaining. This is great!" Luna smacked me in the arm as she bounced beside me, swaying her hips to the terrible beat of whatever the hell was blaring from the speakers. "I mean, come on. You can't be grumpy when you see that. She looks so happy."

Luna clasped her hands to her chest, hearts in her eyes as she looked across the dance floor to Evan, who was currently slow dancing with some punk-ass fourteen-year-old kid with too much gel in his hair.

"I absolutely can when I'm watching my baby girl get felt up by a walking hormone."

"She's not being felt up! They're just dancing," she said dreamily. She was so over-the-moon that Evan had been asked out by the boy she'd apparently been crushing on for some time now, that she couldn't see what was happening right in front of our faces.

"His hand is far too close to her ass. I'm going to break that shit up now."

Luna latched onto my wrist when I started in their direction, using my own momentum to spin me around. She latched on like a spider monkey, lifting up on the toes of her sexy heels and wrapping her arms around my neck.

"You are *not* going to ruin this night for her, Nathanial

Desmond Warren," she scolded, pulling a Georgia Warren and middle-naming me. "Evan has a good head on her shoulders and knows how to make smart decisions. And besides that, Kenneth knows good and well we're both here to chaperone, and after you put the fear of God into him back at the house, I don't think he's brave enough to make a move like that."

I smiled unrepentantly as I wrapped my arms around Luna's waist and pulled her to me. "All right, I'll loosen up. *A little*," I stressed when she smiled brightly. "But I'm not changing my mind on the other thing. She's not allowed to go on actual dates, unchaperoned, until she's sixteen."

Luna nodded solemnly. "Agreed. Now dance with me already before I have to resort to finding a walking hormone of my own to take me for a spin on the dance floor."

We started swaying as the music changed to something slower. "Do you have any clue how much I love you?"

She twisted her lips to the side in mock contemplation. "I might have an idea."

I shook my head. "You couldn't possibly. Because every day I wake up even more in love with you than the day before."

Those tawny eyes twinkled beneath the tacky glow

coming from the disco ball over the dance floor. "Well that's really good. Because I accidentally found the engagement ring you've been keeping in your sock drawer, and my answer is yes."

The End.

Discover Other Books by Jessica

<u>WHITECAP SERIES</u>

Crossing the Line

My Perfect Enemy

<u>WHISKEY DOLLS SERIES</u>

Bombshell

Knockout

Stunner

Seductress

Temptress

<u>HOPE VALLEY SERIES:</u>

Out of My League

Come Back Home Again

The Best of Me

Wrong Side of the Tracks
Stay With Me
Out of the Darkness
The Second Time Around
Waiting for Forever
Love to Hate You
Playing for Keeps
When You Least Expect It
Never for Him

REDEMPTION SERIES

Bad Alibi
Crazy Beautiful
Bittersweet
Guilty Pleasure
Wallflower
Blurred Line
Slow Burn
Favorite Mistake

THE PICKING UP THE PIECES SERIES:

Picking up the Pieces
Rising from the Ashes
Pushing the Boundaries
Worth the Wait

THE COLORS NOVELS:
Scattered Colors
Shrinking Violet
Love Hate Relationship
Wildflower

THE LOCKLAINE BOYS (a LOVE HATE RELATIONSHIP spinoff):
Fire & Ice
Opposites Attract
Almost Perfect

THE PEMBROOKE SERIES (a WILDFLOWER spinoff):
Sweet Sunshine
Coming Full Circle
A Broken Soul

CIVIL CORRUPTION SERIES
Corrupt
Defile
Consume
Ravage

GIRL TALK SERIES:
Seducing Lola

Tempting Sophia
Enticing Daphne
Charming Fiona

<u>STANDALONE TITLES:</u>
One Knight Stand
Chance Encounters
Nightmares from Within

<u>DEADLY LOVE SERIES:</u>
Destructive
Addictive

About Jessica

Born and raised around Houston, Jessica is a self proclaimed caffeine addict, connoisseur of inexpensive wine, and the worst driver in the state of Texas. In addition to being all of these things, she's first and foremost a wife and mom.

Growing up, she shared her mom and grandmother's love of reading. But where they leaned toward murder mysteries, Jessica was obsessed with all things romance.

When she's not nose deep in her next manuscript, you can usually find her with her kindle in hand.

Connect with Jessica now
Website: www.authorjessicaprince.com
Jessica's Princesses Reader Group
Newsletter
Instagram
Facebook
authorjessicaprince@gmail.com

www.ingramcontent.com/pod-product-compliance
Lightning Source LLC
Chambersburg PA
CBHW020911060726
47591CB00004B/1184